'...the Irish Job...'

Frank C. Golden

ISBN: 978-1-913275-65-5

This book was published in cooperation with

Choice Publishing, Drogheda, Co. Louth,

Republic of Ireland.

www.choicepublishing.ie

Front cover image by Bartosz Murzicz

The Author

Frank Golden had a chequered career, as chef, salesman and marketer, before settling down to the life of Barrister and Law Lecturer. A Dubliner, he has read extensively around the period covered in this novel and has drawn on the experiences of his father, who was one of 'Collins's men' in Dublin Castle.

'Once men lose all grip on reality there seems to be no limit to the hatred and passion and rage they can dredge up from their psychological depths, horror which normally we use all of our social institutions to check. Unleashed nationalism on the contrary removes the checks .....'

Barbara Ward, Historian (1914 - 1981)

FOREWORD

The months from December 1919 until the end of November 1921 are now generally regarded in Ireland as the period of *The Irish War of Independence*. However, in January 1919, the opening shots of that conflict were fired in the rural south-west of the country without the prior knowledge or approval of *Irish Volunteer* H.Q. in Dublin. There, a group of local Volunteers successfully ambushed the delivery of a small consignment of gelignite. The explosive sticks were packed in timber boxes and carried on a two-wheeled horse cart on its way to a quarry. As usual with such deliveries, the workmen were accompanied by an armed constable of the *Royal Irish Constabulary (R.I.C.)*. In this, the first engagement of Irish Republicans with the R.I.C. since the 1916 Rising, the constable was shot dead.

The R.I.C. was a country-wide constabulary and totally separate from the *Dublin Metropolitan Police*. It differed in one significant respect from the D.M.P. and the various constabularies of England, Scotland and Wales. R.I.C. constables were armed when on night patrols in the countryside, when attending at evictions and when escorting certain magistrates to and from Court. In the early days, some constables carried either single-shot pistols or muskets. By the 1860's, these firearms became obsolete. Revolvers holding 5 or 6 bullets replaced the old pistols and single shot carbines replaced the musket. The new firearms were quicker to reload, more accurate and they also had a longer range of fire. By the turn of the 19th century the carbines had been replaced with rifles which held a magazine of bullets.

With the establishment of the *Irish Free State* in early 1921, a new civil police force, *An Garda Siochana* (Guardians of the Peace) was established in place of the R.I.C. From the outset, a policy decision was made that *An Garda Siochana* would be an unarmed body when on normal duties. That policy remains in place to this day.

In Ireland until about 1956, the period 1919 to 1923 was colloquially referred to as 'The Troubles' by the then older generation. I certainly recall, in my youth, that many who had been born in the last decades of the 19th century always referred to the 1916 Republican insurrection in Dublin as *'The Rebellion'*. However, in the years following the 1956 Hungarian uprising against its puppet Soviet government, the term *'The 1916 Rising'* gradually came into common usage and remained so until 1966, the bicentenary of The 1916 Rising. In that year, many commemorative events took place throughout the country. Thereafter, in Ireland, the composite term for the period 1919-1921 has been *The War of Independence*.

It is my belief that during that conflict, the Irish 'side' had the advantage both in Intelligence and in international propaganda from late 1919 until the Truce of 1921. In London, Sam Maguire was privy to much of the thinking – and more? – of the *'Irish Section'* of Scotland Yard. An Irish Protestant from Co. Cork, he was also the I.R.B. 'Head Centre' for London and the South East of England. In Ireland, Michael Collins was the 'Head Centre' of a country-wide Intelligence service using the reactivated network of secret Irish Republican

Brotherhood (I.R.B.) 'Centres' within the Irish Volunteers and the Sinn Féin organisation. However, from January 1920 until the British withdrawal from Southern Ireland in 1922, Michael Collins had a 'top agent' in Dublin Castle. This man was Clerk-Assistant (C.A.) to Andy (Alfred) Cope. Earlier in his career, Cope had been a *Customs and Excise* sleuth. Once, posing as a docker, he had insinuated himself into a smuggling gang operating in the Thames docks areas. Had they found him out to be a 'Revenue man', he would have ended up in the Thames with his throat slit. Later in his career, he had spent some years in Ireland visiting the countryside. Posing as an ornithologist, carrying a telescope and dressed in tweed plus-fours and deerstalker hat, he cycled around remote country areas. On spotting a faint column of smoke in uninhabited terrain, he would note its location on an Ordnance Survey map. A month or so later, the Royal Irish Constabulary would descend on the hapless 'moonshiners'.

In 1919, when in early retirement, Cope was an active member of his local Liberal Party branch. By then, Prime Minister Lloyd George had become dissatisfied with one of the two joint Under Secretaries, the most senior officials in the Administration at Dublin Castle, both of whom were answerable to the Viceroy and Governor General of Ireland. One, an upper class Roman Catholic, was an unofficial and discreet Government contact point with the Irish Roman Catholic hierarchy. The second, the focus of Lloyd George's ire, was pensioned off. Cope was offered the job, and accepted. Henceforth, Cope would be the key Under Secretary dealing with administration and correspondence.

My father, Bernard James Golden (1880-1973) was appointed Clerk Assistant to Cope in early 1920. He served in that role until Michael Collins officially entered Dublin Castle to take over the reins of power in 1922. From the first day he took up his post, his duties – as instructed by Cope – included opening every single envelope arriving in Dublin Castle, no matter to whom it was addressed. When all had been scrutinised by Cope and notes taken of particular correspondence, my father would then re-seal the envelopes in such a way as to leave no trace of interference. They would then be delivered by Castle messenger to their designated recipients.

In those days and until the early 1950s, all civil servants and employees in every trade and profession worked a five and a half day week. Many employees returned home for lunch – or 'dinner' as it was commonly called. On his way home, my father would meet one of Michael Collins's inner circle and convey to him the day's crucial intelligence items.

The Irish propaganda campaign was a world-wide one throughout the Empire, in Europe and most especially in the U.S.A. where the Irish Diaspora was well organised and cohesive. The I.R.B.'s relationship with its cousin organisation there, *Clan na Gael*, was longstanding and very close. Most importantly, *Clan* was a constant source of funds for Irish Republicans. It was in regular contact with certain U.S. Democrats - not all of whom had Irish roots – and so had some indirect influence in the political scene there.

As regards the situation in Ireland at that time, it has to be said that direct engagements between the ill-armed Irish Volunteers and the British army were few and far between. On the English side, ironically, Lloyd George did not wish to employ a direct military force for good geo-political reasons. Instead, he introduced a temporary policy force to assist the R.I.C. This was the 'Auxiliary Division' Royal Irish Constabulary. The senior grades of this force were largely composed of former officers of the British Army, many of whom would have attended minor public schools or grammar schools. Few had ever attended Military Academy. Most held 'field commissions' which, of course, lapsed at the end of the First World War.

The term *Irish Republican Army* was eschewed by the successor organisation to the *National Volunteers* of the 1916 Easter Rising, the *Irish Volunteers*. The original I.R.A. was a group of former Irish officers and soldiers who had been in the Union Army during the American Civil War. Following that, they staged an invasion of Canada and were routed with the loss of one man by a local Canadian militia unit.

PROLOGUE

'The Irish job is a policeman's job and if we have to use the Army we shall have failed.'

Lloyd George, December 1919

Thomas Jones (Cabinet Secretary) Whitehall Diary,

Vol. 3, p. 73

France, Autumn 1915.

'Ready, are we then, gentlemen?'

Sitting at a worn table in the musty dining-room of the abandoned house, the middle-aged major tapped his cigarette ash onto a cracked saucer. Eyebrows raised, he glanced at the captain flanking him on the right and the subaltern to his left.

'Yes Sir,' they intoned.

Though the second-lieutenant's assent seemed spontaneous, the major caught the fractional delay in his response. Still in his late teens and patently unsure of himself, he was clearly a Military Academy chap and not one of those Johnny-come-lately fellows holding a bare Field Commission. The captain, a man in his late twenties, bore himself with composure.

'And the Judge Advocate's Officer...'

He glanced towards the bespectacled officer leafing through the Charge Sheets at a spindly hall table to the right. 'Captain Cromie...yes?'

'Yes, Major Ridgeway, Sir. Everything is in order.'

'Good! Now then...' the Major paused, finger zig-zagging down a foolscap sheet. 'Ah! Yes, the first prisoner today I see is Private John Mernagh. Is he present?'

'He is, Sir, yes, and is now under guard in the wine cellar below.'

'Which, I presume, is otherwise empty?'

They chuckled dutifully at the laboured witticism.

'Indeed, Sir, yes.'

'Captain, how long will these proceedings take?'

'All the charges ought to be disposed of by lunchtime, Sir.'

'Good.'

Turning, the Major addressed the nervous subaltern sitting on a rickety cane chair.

'Now then, Lieutenant ... Lieutenant Waite, is it?'

'Yes, Sir!'

Waite shot to his feet.

'And you are the Prisoner's Friend in these proceedings?'

'Yes, Sir.'

'Have you ever before served on a Court Martial?'

'No, Sir, I have not.'

'Do you know what is expected of you? And have you met your charge?'

'Yes, Sir and I have spoken with him.'

Hesitating, he remained standing, uncertain. However, as the Major turned away and took a last draw on his cigarette, Waite sat down.

'Now before I formally open this tribunal, I have to remind all of you gentlemen that, whether in barracks, bell tent or premises such as these – not withstanding their decrepit state – the judicial proceedings about to commence are regularly constituted and are fully in accordance with Military Law. It is, therefore, a properly convened Field Court Martial. Furthermore, with the King's Regulations duly observed, this Tribunal has full powers of all military punishment up to and including the imposition of the death penalty. Is that understood, gentlemen?'

'Yes Sir,' they chorused.

'Then let us get on with it.'

Drawing his Webley from its holster, he tapped the pistol on the worn, grain-ribbed kitchen table.

'I now declare this general Field Court Martial in session. Proceed, Captain Cromie.'

'Yes Major, Sir.' Glancing down at the file in his hand, he continued. 'There are eleven charges to be heard today, the first being the most serious. It borders on mutiny and insubordination. I understand that both the Company O.C. who initially investigated the case and the Battalion O.C. who considered that officer's report were uncertain as to which charge ought to be preferred. The latter therefore decided to combine both offences as Cowardice and Refusal to obey an officer's command.'

'All offences were committed in the field?'

'Yes, Sir.'

'And the command was lawfully given?'

'Yes, Sir.'

'Good. And the remaining charges?'

'All are minor A.F.(252) Offences: two pilfering and eight disciplinary.'

'Well then as the gravest charge is of a capital nature we shall deal with it first. Who is the Prisoner and what is his regiment and rank?'

'He...' Cromie paused, peering at the Charge Sheet ... 'he is a sixteen year-old Private John or Jack Mernagh of the Royal Liverpool Rifles who volunteered a year ago and ...'

'Did you say he is sixteen years of age?'

'I did, Sir, yes.'

Major Ridgeway grimaced. 'Before we proceed further, as Tribunal President I have to remind all of you serving on it – including you as the Prisoner's Friend, Mr. Waite – that the age of the prisoner is not a relevant issue in this, a military court. Although the minimum enlistment age for soldiers is eighteen years of age, we all know that for generations boys have lied as to their age in their eagerness to become soldiers – or indeed sailors. And such has been the case in armies and navies the world over. Many such rascals became excellent soldiers. Indeed, today's outstanding example is that of our own Chief, General Robertson. However, once a fit and sane young man is properly enlisted, his age is an irrelevance insofar as Military Law and Regulations are concerned. Such a man is subject to all their penal consequences inasmuch as they apply. And they apply no less to boy soldiers than they do to the rest of us. Is that understood, gentlemen?'

'Yes, Sir,' they chorused in weary unison.

'Good! Proceed then, Captain Cromie.'

'Yes, Sir!'

Turning he glanced at the N.C.O. standing ramrod rigid at the door.

'Sergeant, fetch the prisoner'.

Waite shifted on his seat, nerving himself for his first involvement at a military trial – or at any trial for that matter. That had certainly been the last thing on his mind as he took a seat in the half-filled brigade mess the previous evening.

ooooo0000000ooooo

'Mind if I join you, Lieutenant?'

Absorbed in the mess menu, Waite was somewhat taken aback on the approach of a captain. Dropping the quarto sheet and rising, he whipped his right hand in salute.

'No need for quite that formality, Lieutenant. In the Officers' Mess all caps are off and we are all at ease ... well to a certain extent.' Drawing out a chair, he introduced himself. 'Cromie, Field Provost Marshall's unit.' Beaming, he smoothed his red-gold moustache.

'How do you do, Sir?'

'Very well, thank you, Lieutenant...?'

'Oh! Sorry, Sir! Waite is the name.'

'Well then, Waite, is there a Mess Orderly about?'

'I've just caught his eye, Sir, and he's on his way.'

As Cromie dictated his choice, it puzzled Waite as to why, with several vacant tables about, a Captain would choose to dine with a junior officer. His affable manner seemed somewhat odd for a Provost Marshall Officer. He had heard that such fellows were very keen in fault-finding. But then how would he, a temporary second lieutenant with a bare field promotion, be familiar with the niceties of protocol in an officer's mess?

The captain had now lit a cigarette and was exhaling, his eyes sharp behind rimless spectacles. 'You're Indian Army, I see.'

'Yes Sir.'

'And your regiment is...?'

'131st Baluchistan Rifles, Sir. We are stationed close to La Basse.'

'Really! That's at least twenty miles away from here. What has you here at this brigade H.Q?' Cromie stubbed out his half-smoked cigarette.

'I was discharged from the Field Hospital at Étaples two days ago, Sir, certified fit for duty.'

'When does your recuperation leave expire?'

'Today, Sir. I am now returning to my unit.'

'So, you stopped a Hun bullet?'

'No, Sir. It actually passed clean through my shoulder.'

Cromie chuckled. 'I didn't mean that literally, Waite. Where did it get you?'

'It grazed my collar-bone and an infection set in.'

'So you were first given the iodine treatment in the trenches?'

'Yes, Sir. The medicos told me I shall always have a bit of a stiff shoulder – especially in rather cold weather.'

The captain laughed. 'Well then a good job it wasn't your sword arm.' He prodded the dish set before him.

Waite smiled at the captain's jest. He seemed a good sort.

'Now then, Lieutenant, let me see your papers?' His tone was sharp.

'No, Sir ... I mean yes, Sir.'

Caught off-balance, Waite fumbled in his tunic pocket. Removing the Regimental Medical Officer's certificate and his travel warrant from his pocket-book, he handed them both across the table. As the captain scrutinised them, Waite felt a tinge of anxiety. Had he transgressed some army rule or regulation? That was easily done as no wartime soldier holding a temporary promotion to officer level was given the time to read the plethora of Army Regulations issued him in the few short months of his officer training course.

Removing his spectacles, Cromie nudged the papers across the table.

'Well, these seem to be in order. I am satisfied that you are not a deserter posing as an officer.'

'I beg your pardon, Sir!'

Smiling at Waite's look of incredulity, the captain continued. 'Ah, yes indeed. There have been some imposters already. Inevitable really, given the ragbag influx of civilians conscripted into a wartime army. Some never take to military discipline. As you will have probably gathered by now, military offences are my business. Well, that is, for the moment. In fact, tomorrow morning I shall be the prosecuting officer at a Court Martial. But deuced if the subaltern I had chosen to have with me hasn't gone down with of, all things, appendicitis! And of course he was but the one junior officer to spare at Brigade H.Q. So I had resigned myself to the bother of finding a suitable replacement at battalion level closer to the trial venue. And then - most fortuitously - now I find you here as that replacement and one that I can nab, so to speak.'

Stung by Cromie's jibe at civilian volunteers, Waite asserted himself. 'Nab, sir!'

Cromie smiled. 'I do apologise, Mr. Waite, for the levity. But you see you're an ideal choice in that, being a second lieutenant, you are closest to other ranks for court martial duty.'

'But Sir, am I not under continuing Royal Army Medical Corps ...'

'Jurisdiction?'

'Thank you, Sir, yes.'

'Well it says here that you are '*Fit for Duty.*' Peering closely at the document, he continued, 'This is signed by - dreadful handwriting - ... yes, a Surgeon Major H. - *Park* - is it?'

'Yes, Sir, it is.'

'Well then, this means you're now out of RAMC jurisdiction. And as you have not yet returned to your regiment, I have the authority to impress you for Field Courts Martial duty.' He paused, smiling. 'Or 'nab you', as I somewhat flippantly put it.'

'But Sir, I know nothing about Court Martials.'

'Courts Martial, Waite. To be pedantic, the operative noun is Court with Martial the adjective. Anyway, have no fear, you won't be serving on the tribunal itself. You see, one of the soldiers charged has requested a Prisoner's Friend – as he is so entitled, and you, Waite, fit the bill for that role.

'You mean, Sir, a soldier under charge may ask for someone to defend him?'

'Well, not quite that. You see this is an Army-appointed 'Friend'.'

'Surely that would be some kind of a lawyer, Sir?'

'Good Heavens man, no! This is an army trial, not an Old Bailey one. And in case you have forgotten, there's a war on. Soldiers don't expect to be mollycoddled in peace time and they know there's not a chance of that in war.'

'Where, may I enquire, is this court martial to be held?'

'Oh, about twenty miles from here, I'd say. Not too far from La Basse. It will be held in what's left of the village of Colombey l'Eglise St. Molay. The venue is, I believe, in the surviving half of the local padre's house. The church there survived the Revolution and then the Franco-Prussian War in 1870. However, early on in this war, all the villagers fled in fear of the advancing Boche, and the whole place was hammered to rubble by their artillery. Yet, for whatever reason, their gunners spared the padre's house. It seems the Hun had advanced a salient too far from their frontline so they withdrew shortly afterwards. When our advancing forces regained the village, this house was requisitioned for army use. He eyed Waite quizzically. 'Next question?'

'How, Sir, shall I return to my company following the Court Martial?' Waite ventured.

'Well, the proceedings ought to end before lunchtime as – thankfully - Major Ridgeway is presiding. In civvy street, I understand he was a solicitor with a thriving practice. When the war broke out, he – though a little on in years – volunteered to serve but was rejected. And so,' Cromie chuckled, 'he enlisted as a Private! Point made, the Army promptly assigned him to Courts Martial duties. A thoroughly nice man, but far too soft for soldiering. So, other than the trial of the prisoner whose *Friend* you will be, most of tomorrow's cases are minor offences, so you'll have plenty of time to return to your unit.'

'Walking...Sir?'

'Of course not, Waite. I shall have the use of a staff car for the day and, as I will be up to my neck in paperwork afterwards, I will have my driver take you there. Anything else?'

'I think not, Sir, – oh yes, there is one thing more.'

Cromie sighed. 'And that is?'

'I still know nothing about the duties of a *Prisoner's Friend.*'

'You shall, Waite. Where are you billeted tonight?'

'In Madame d'Armont's Chateau.'

Cromie grinned.

'Is that what Charlotte calls it now?'

Waite was on the defensive. 'It is on the Brigade Adjutant's approved list for officers' lodgings.'

'I *do* know that. I visited the bally place when the list was being drawn up. It's no more than a large house with some parkland – hardly a chateau. Anyway when I return to my quarters, I shall have an orderly take you my copy of Brigade's *Officers' Guide to Field Courts Martial.* That covers all you will need to know as to the ... eh ... the duties of a Prisoner's Friend – and that is not much. So do study it carefully and return it to me in the morning.'

'I shall do that, Sir, yes. And thank you.'

'When you've finished your meal, you will have a busy couple of hours reading tonight. Now, is there anything else I need to explain?'

'Just one matter ... who is it, Sir, that I am ... *befriending?*'

'Oh, some young fool who joined the army in a boyish fit of enthusiasm and then found it all rather unpleasant. His plea, it seems, is that he had not deserted but was caring for a wounded 'mate'.'

Waite, frowned. 'When you say boyish, Sir, how old is he?'

Waite pushed his plate away and lit another cigarette. 'Oh, fifteen or sixteen, I believe.'

Waite was incredulous. 'But he's only a boy. Surely that can't be lawful?'

Cromie smiled. 'Oh, yes it is! That is, under Military Law. The Army shows neither fear nor favour to anyone who insists on joining up. You may well be correct as to the overall legality of this but until somebody challenges that in a court of law, our military betters will continue to use their skills in the service of the Crown.' Pausing, he added. 'And so, there we are. Anything else on your mind?'

'No sir,' Waite replied, still somewhat shocked.

'Good! My driver will pick you up at eight a.m. sharp in the morning.'

'Yes, Sir.'

'Well now, I must away.'

As Captain Cromie strode off, Waite had the distinct impression that he had been manoeuvred by an expert. What had he let himself in for?

Chapter 1

"Any attempt at secession will be fought with the same determination ... resources (and) resolve as the northern States of America put into the fight against the southern States. It is important that that should be known not merely throughout the world but in Ireland itself.'

Lloyd George, Parliamentary Debates, H.O.C. Vol. 123, No. 6162, Col. 694.

1

Roscrea-Parsonstown Road, King's County, 21 February 1920.

'It's freezing cold.'

What with the rushing head wind and the roar of the army lorry's big engine, Jack couldn't make out what his companion was saying.

'Can't hear you, Stan, what did you say?'

Shouting this time, the young private's voice barely carried. 'It's freezing cold, Jack, can't you slow down a bit?'

'No. I want to get back to the barracks before the light begins to fade.' Jack Dougherty – as Jack Mernagh called himself now – had little sympathy for Stan's whining. 'I want to get back before dark otherwise we'll be easy targets for the Shinners. Whatever chance we have in daytime, we're finished if they ambush us at night. So you keep watching out ahead like you were told for anything that looks like trouble and then use that rifle when I say.'

Though not a particularly windy day, the speed of the big opened-fronted GMC lorry converted a light breeze from the north-west into a bone-chilling gale. Each man, although buttoned up to the neck in army greatcoats, with woollen gloves and caps pulled over their ears, still got the brunt of the biting cold air. Stan, a recent recruit, was part of an incoming regiment replacing Jack's Munster Fusiliers, one of the last Irish regiments soon to be posted somewhere in the Empire or the Middle East, well away from the growing 'Troubles' in Ireland.

Stan clapped his hands together for warmth. 'Me hands are freezing, Jack. The rifle barrel is as cold as ice.'

'Then stop holding the bally thing between your knees and prop it against the door. It won't fall out.' Jack bit back his impatience for the soft recruit who had no idea what hell men had gone through in the war. Wet cold muddy trenches didn't spare you from mortars, shrapnel or the sniper's bullet. Nor that one shell which could wipe you and your mates off the face of the earth before its whistling whine reached your ears. Stan would have to learn to survive a lot worse than cold weather.

Ten minutes later Stan was at it again. 'How far ahead is Birr now, Jack?'

'We're more than three quarters the way back now, you can put up with that, can't you.'

'Yeah, I suppose so.'

Stan wasn't to know that any time now the army would lose both lorry and its load of full petroleum tins. O'Reilly had assured Jack there'd be no shooting if they surrendered as ordered. Well, he'd make damn sure Stan did just that.

Driving out of Crinkle Barracks in Birr just after 8a.m. that morning, it was a good sign that, despite the cold weather, a bright winter sun shone in the blue sky. Thinking back over all the time he'd spent deserting and re-enlisting in the British Army under different names and in various regiments since the Étaples Mutiny, Jack had to admit that, all said, his time with Percy Toplis had been well spent. He had learned a lot, and had even managed to put aside a few bob. Yeah, since then, things had worked out well. After the mutiny, he had had no problem getting back to England and then returning to Ireland.

3

He had headed for Cork where nobody would know him and enlisted in the Munster Fusiliers – his third re-enlistment so far since the Armistice. It was easy now. With the war well over, the army redcaps weren't as fussy as they had been. But he had no intention of going along with his latest regiment on their next posting to one or other of the trouble spots in the Empire or its new territories in Mesopotamia, India or wherever. The time had come to depart, this time for good. So today would be his last in the British Army. He'd been waiting since last year for the best opportunity to 'jump ship' and that had come a couple of months ago. It was that chance meeting with Mr. Bernard O'Reilly. Or was it a chance meeting? O'Reilly, a man in his forties, had been an army schoolmaster since before the war, qualified to give instruction in the Three Rs to intelligent but half-educated men who had taken the 'King's shilling' and would benefit from more schooling. Later, they would remain in the army doing the paperwork – clerks when all is said and done.

Jack had no need of O'Reilly's classes. He had left Trim Reformatory at fourteen going on fifteen with a good National School education behind him. He knew how to read, write, spell and do sums, fractions, division, long division, multiplication and decimals. And in sixth class they had had to write simple letters and learn off French and Latin verbs. But, after all that, he had ended up as a farm labourer with that mean old bastard of an uncle.

He had seen O'Reilly around the barracks but had no cause to meet him until one night in the local pub. Jack's mates, knowing he was a non-drinker, didn't expect him to pay for a 'round' of beer but they kept buying him lemonade until he was full to the gills with the stuff. On his third visit to the lavatory, O'Reilly came in. When the drunk between them had left, O'Reilly spoke. 'You don't drink, do you?'

'No, Sir. Never did.' Jack glanced sideways.

O'Reilly was holding a lighted match over the bowl of his pipe. 'And you're in the Munster Fusiliers?'

'Yes, Sir.' Wary now, Jack waited. What was he after? Buttoning up, he turned around. O'Reilly, now facing the door, was pulling his pipe to a slow burn. 'How long are you signed up for?'

'Five years. Then on the Reserve.'

'How would you like to leave the army safely and get a good civilian job?'

Jack thought quickly before replying. 'I'd be interested. But how could I do that?'

'What's your name?'

'Jack Dougherty, Sir.'

'Well, Jack, we can't talk right now. But we'll meet again soon in a safer place. I'll get in contact with you one day next week.'

O'Reilly had made contact the following Thursday. The tiny note he had slipped to him instructed Jack to return to the church following Mass parade the following Sunday and ... Jack stiffened. Something was blocking the road in the distance! Yes, this was it – the ambush!

oooo0000ooooo

London

Pushing his chair away from the small writing table, Sam Maguire moved his head from side to side, loosening his stiff neck muscles. He shuffled the five sealed and addressed OHMS envelopes. They would have uninterrupted passage through the postal system of Great Britain and Ireland. Not one Special Branch detective along the way would give them a second glance.

Lighting up, he drew deeply on the cigarette and, idly glancing about the sitting room of his South London lodgings, he focussed on the large gilt-framed photograph above the mantle shelf from which frowned H.M. King George V. Smiling faintly, he recalled that, as his landlady first showed him to his room, he had stopped before the portrait, straightened and briefly bowed his head. That she immediately took to be the obeisance of a loyal subject and, as he had intended, it had consolidated her belief in his loyalty to the Crown. Later on, when he had settled in, after what she imagined to be discreet questioning, she was impressed to learn that, apart from being an Irish Protestant, he was a senior official in the London Post Office. He had further copper-fastened her trust with occasional hints as to the confidential aspects of his Government duties concerning the suppression of the current Sinn Féin unrest in Ireland and its threat to the peace of the United Kingdom. Her support was cemented when she had noted his masonic regalia in his wardrobe. Kenneth, her dear departed husband, she confided, had been a member of the local Lodge – and thank goodness for that! As a Mason's widow, she could count on the order's support for the rest of her life.

She was especially solicitous in respect of his letters when he was away. She learned that, in the course of his Post Office duties, he was frequently absent from London, either travelling on the London-Holyhead train or on the Mail Boat to or from Dublin. When he was away, she carefully separated his letters from the morning post and left them in his room. When an OHMS envelope was delivered by hand she would hand them to him with some ceremony and a knowing smile. Sam had confided that the elderly men who delivered them were government messengers. Little did she know that they were tried and trusted Brothers in the Organisation, all now retired from their various lawful employments. No-one would give such old fellows a second glance. Smiling to himself, he recalled being told by the oldest of them, a saintly patriarch with a beard, that he had been involved in the 1880's bombing campaign in England.

Glancing at the envelopes, he checked once again that the Dublin addresses on each were correct. The Organisation had long perfected a secure courier system using the Post Office service on the Holyhead/Kingstown Mail Boat which ensured delivery in Dublin early the next day. Today's envelopes contained typed or written abstracts of cables telegraphed from America – mainly from New York – to 'safe' commercial addresses in London, each in a mixture of clear language, business code and cipher, universally accepted to protect trade secrecy. The cables he received from America were usually from Mr. de Valera, all of whose letters were code-addressed to the Dáil Éireann Cabinet and related to his fundraising activities in the U.S.A. As President of Dáil Éireann and an American born citizen, de Valera had no problem travelling around the United States promoting the sale of Irish Republic Certificates.

In his capacity as Head Centre of the Irish Republican Brotherhood for London and Southern England, Maguire was required to deal with a myriad of clandestine matters. Dáil Éireann delegates and emissaries were continually making representations in various capitals of Europe and further overseas, with the result that many coded cables and post arrived daily in London for secure conveyance to Dublin. Most of them dealt with matters as varied as Dáil emissaries' reports, foreign press treatment of Irish affairs, progress on weapons and munitions procurement in Europe, as well as trade issues. And of course there were matters relating to the proscribed *Irish Bulletin,* with its circulated copies posted from London. Most clandestine correspondence arrived weekly at different London addresses, the homes of IRB men working or retired in the capital. The Organisation's long-established communication procedures were known only to the handful of Brothers who were engaged in ciphering and deciphering. Many of them had been Royal Navy telegraphists. But when it came to his own confidential exchanges with John Devoy, the veteran Fenian who ran the American branch of the Organisation in New York, no one else was involved.

Stretching to his full height, Sam Maguire flexed his shoulders, then settled back again at the table to deal with more Intelligence items for Mick Collins in Dublin.

ooooOOOOooooo

London, 21 February, 1920

Kate Swanton alighted from the motor cab and paid the driver.

Going through the motions of searching inside her handbag, she waited until the cab had moved away and merged with the traffic. She had been warned that many of the taxicab men had been members of the London Metropolitan Police until they had taken part in the first ever police strike in 1918 when they had been sacked. But for all that, she knew many of them were, with some justification, suspected of keeping up contact with those still employed in the Force. She walked the few paces to the final bank on her list. Inside, she glanced around. There was little to distinguish it from the five she had visited since the morning. Small queues waited a little distance away from the counters. Choosing the shortest queue, she waited, outwardly composed and relaxed. It was nearly closing time.

The teller beckoned her forward. 'Good afternoon,' she smiled.

'Good afternoon, miss. May I be of assistance?'

'I wish to change four pounds for sovereigns, if I may?'

'Certainly, Miss.'

Nudging forward the envelope containing the four new one pound notes under the brass grill, she waited. As he removed them, the teller held each one up to the light. How diligent, she reflected, he was the first to check that they were not counterfeit.

As he continued flattening out and adding the notes to a bundle, the teller assessed the young lady. Though clearly Irish, she was a well-spoken person. The notes were in a good quality envelope and he concluded that, though not a regular bank customer here, she was nonetheless a genuine one. Yet, for all that, bank tellers had been warned to be especially vigilant in transactions involving the exchange of bank notes for gold sovereigns.

'You did say sovereigns, Miss?' he asked.

Apprehensive now, wary, Kate nodded. 'Yes indeed.'

'You do know, Miss, that sovereigns are not very practical for daily purchases? So why not use the higher value silver pieces?'

Kate smiled. 'Precisely because these sovereigns are not required for the purchase of shop goods – that is, in the ordinary sense.'

'I don't quite understand what you mean, Miss?'

'Well, it is quite simple. You see, tomorrow, I shall be accompanying my elderly aunt to an antique furniture auction in Redhill – an executor's sale, in fact. As I'm sure you well know, cheques are only accepted in payment at public auctions if the bidder is known to or has been vouched for the auctioneer. So my Aunt is most insistent as to the exact number of sovereigns I am to hold for her there. Of course,' she paused, 'should your chief cashier wish to have her name and address together with that of the auctioneer, perhaps I ought to deal with him?'

Concluding that her explanation was reasonable enough to satisfy any bank manager and that she presented as a thoroughly respectable young lady, he reached across to the tray holding the sovereigns.

'I didn't mean to pry, Miss,' he said, 'I hope you understand.'

'But of course you didn't,' Kate smiled at him. As he pushed the four gold sovereigns under the grill, she relaxed. Opening her small handbag, she slipped them inside. They would join the rest in the chamois purse later. Bidding the teller a polite good-day, she left the bank and hailed a cab.

'St. Pancras Station Hotel, please,' she said. As she stepped into the back of the car, she smiled inwardly. A total of thirty eight pounds had been exchanged for sovereigns. It had been a good day.

ooooo0000ooooo

Waite stopped outside the house in Victoria Street and checked his notebook. Yes, this was the number. Pulling the brass doorbell, he looked about as he waited. The noiseless opening of the door caught him off guard. 'May I help you?' a middle-aged man in servant's attire waited.

'I have an appointment at Flat 3b at 10a.m.'

'Your name, Sir?'

'Waite.'

'Please come in, Captain Waite, the major is expecting you. I am Sergeant Scovel.'

Following him up the staircase, Waite paused as Scovel opened one of the three doors on the first floor landing. Inside, the decor was stolid Victorian, a dark sombre carpet of indeterminate hue was complemented by embossed dark green wallpaper. In the gloom, the few fading wall prints of Highland

11

scenes were anything but cheering. The sergeant stopped at an inner door and tapped twice.

'Show Captain Waite in please, Scovel,' a muffled voice replied.

Entering a large, brilliantly lit room, Waite was momentarily dazzled by the single glaring electric light bulb hanging from the ceiling. Directly below that, a civilian, head bowed, sat at a large desk, strewn with manila folders and papers. Without looking up, he dismissed Scovel. 'Thank you, sergeant. That will be all for the moment.'

As the door closed, the major put down his pen and looked up. Astonished, Waite couldn't believe his eyes. It was the prosecutor at that Irishman's court martial! What the dickens was his name?

'Well, well, well, if it isn't Waite of Heliopolis! The intrepid Waite, if I am to believe Colonel Meinertzhagen.'

He stood and strode forward, hand outstretched. Waite, momentarily speechless, racked his memory for the officer's name. Yes! He had it. 'Major Crombie, Sir, how do you do?'

'Oh dear, Waite, off on the wrong foot already, are we? Cromie it was and Cromie it remains, please.'

'I do apologise, major, but it must be five years since we met,' Waite stammered.

'I jest, Waite. We have both encountered many in the Service since then. To tell you the truth, I had also forgotten your name though, I assure you, not you, after your bravura performance at that Court Martial in France. Who would have suspected the callow lieutenant to be a very Solomon! But I am flattered you recalled my name. Well, almost. I understand from Meinertzhagen that you saved his skin in Cairo.'

'That was a lucky accident,' Waite began. He drew breath to elaborate, but Cromie motioned Waite to the chair facing him. 'Do please sit down. I'll be free in a jiffy.'

Looking around, Waite was impressed. Cromie seemed taller and more impressive than he had in France. He had gained weight, but his spectacles remained unchanged and his hair remained a glossy red. Two telephones, files and documents surrounding the blotting pad all but obscured the desk's tooled leather inlay. Glancing about, Waite saw that the furniture was of the Victorian period beloved of his mother. The large button back brown leather Chesterfield with matching arm chairs he guessed were at least forty years old. Major Cromie put down his pen and opened a manila folder. 'Now then, Waite, let's have a look at your file'. Holding it open with one hand, his finger tapped each page as he turned it over.

'You were born in Simla in 1894. Let's see, your early education was by private tutor. Following that, you went to public school in England. When you completed your studies, you returned to India – and then the War broke out and you volunteered to fight.' He smiled at Waite over his glasses. 'I see you received a Governor's Commission in the Indian Army – you must tell me about that sometime. Then, let me see ... attached to the Baluchistan Rifles, you first saw active service in France. A Mons Medal man too, I see! In 1916-17 you were in German East Africa where you are listed as being On Special Service. Now, the Special Service covers a multitude – so what exactly were you up to? And where?' He sat back in his seat and fixed Waite with a penetrating stare.

13

'I was attached to General Dunsterville's Expeditionary Force to the Caucasus,' Waite said.

'Ah! The hush-hush Dunsterforce no less,' Cromie exclaimed. 'A perfectly botched show that was – letting the Reds get their hands on Baku oilfields. What were your duties there?'

'I acted mainly as translator in talks between the British and White Russian officers,' Waite said.

Cromie flipped the pages of the file before him. 'There's no mention of language skills here. Why is that?'

Waite swallowed. 'When I was interviewed for my temporary commission in Simla, no one asked me about language skills, Sir. Once they heard that I had been in the OTC at my public school and could handle a Lee Enfield .303, they seemed satisfied.'

'But how did you achieve such a level of fluency in Russian?

'From a Russian bookseller in Calcutta. You see, his son was a fellow pupil of mine,' Waite answered. 'My father had dealings with him as he was an import/export agent of some kind – my father was a bookseller. Mr Maslinsky was Jewish, and my father agreed that I should help with some domestic chores on their Sabbath – lighting the kitchen stove, filling kettles, small things like that and in return for this kindness, Mr Maslinsky taught me Russian.'

'How old were you then?' Cromie asked.

'About seven or eight, Sir. I continued to assist them until I was twelve.'

'Interesting,' Cromie tilted his chair on its back legs. 'Not unlike the experience of our own C.I.G.S..'

'Sir Henry Wilson?' Waite ventured.

'The same. It seems Sir Henry had private tutors during his childhood in Ireland, all of whom were French. That stood him well when he liaised with Foch and the French General Staff during the war.'

'Sir Henry is Irish?'

'Oh yes, in a manner of speaking.' Cromie smiled. 'But I rather think that, as with Wellington, Sir Henry doesn't like to be reminded of that. Anyway, returning to your war record, I see you next served in Meshed. Doing what?'

'We had wireless telegraphy receivers there and they could pick up every transmission from Moscow – that is why Meshed was chosen as our closest command post to Russia. My task was to translate. Most of it was Bolshevist propaganda masquerading as news but occasionally there were some nugget of real value.'

Cromie's glasses glinted. 'Did you see action there?'

'Not directly, Sir, and as you probably know, if the Russians took prisoners, it was for interrogation first – usually involving torture – and then the poor devils were shot. And I'm afraid some of our people did the same. Especially when those twenty-five Red Commissars were executed.'

'The White Russians shot them, Waite, we didn't.' Cromie retorted. 'Mind you, I can't say I would be overly concerned about anyone shooting a Red Commissar – they were a thoroughly bad lot.' He closed the folder. 'So, do I conclude that you are willing to play your part in combating the Bolshevist menace?'

'Oh yes, Sir,' Waite replied.

'Excellent.' Cromie placed the folder on top of the tottering pile on his desk. 'Well then, with appropriate preparation, you'll be ready to spend a few months in Ireland before that.'

'Ireland?' Waite exclaimed.

'Yes.' Cromie rose. 'You see, the Shinners behind the rebellion there in 1916 have re-grouped and are becoming a nuisance. It's time they were put in their place.' He paused. 'Let's get down to business.'

'Major – sorry Sir, Mr. Cromie,' Waite stammered. 'You do know I spent less than ten days learning some of the ropes, so to speak, in Cairo, following my meeting with Colonel Meinertzagen. I was given to understand that I would be working in Russia.'

'Eventually yes, but that training course was just to familiarise you with basic police detective work involved in political crime. You're not expecting to be a Peeler on the beat for the rest of your life, are you?' Cromie sounded mildly affronted.

'No, Sir. But I really feel I don't know enough to equip me to work against the Bolshevists – or the Shinners.'

'Of course you don't know enough. None of us can ever know enough. One constantly learns on the job, so to speak. However in your case, you will now be attending a few weeks' preparatory instruction course at Stepney Barracks. That will

16

more than equip you for dealing with these people.'

'Shall I be working in Army Intelligence there, Sir?'

'In a sense, yes, but 'with' rather than 'in'.'

'I don't quite understand...'

'Let me explain. Army Intelligence deals with enemy and potential enemy armed forces of England and the Empire. However, internal civilian elements in England such as labour activists, Bolshevist conspirators, anarchists, Irish Nationalists and the like which pose a threat to the political order are dealt with separately by M.I.5, together with the Special Branch at Scotland House in Whitehall. Such political malcontents are only of concern to the Army insofar as they may directly affect it and they are dealt with by the Army's Special Investigation Branch. Indeed, some of the chaps attending the instruction course with you will afterwards be attached to the S.I.B. operating from Army H.Q. in Dublin.

'And which Intelligence body shall I be with, Sir?'

'None that I have mentioned. You will be associated with the G1 element of Section H. That – Section H – is the Army's special Intelligence group which was set up after the Boer War.'

'Really! The Boer War?'

'Oh, yes. Section H – no idea what the 'H' stands for – was established to anticipate new, unexpected threats so that we would never be caught unprepared. Anyway, following the Armistice, plans for a smaller post-War Army resulted in the 'clear out' of a whole rake of special Field and War Office departments. Thankfully though, the Bolshevist menace ensured that Section H remained intact.' He paused. 'Well, that was the idea. Now some of the special duties of Section H involve aspects of military intelligence and secret service activities.'

'But aren't intelligence and secret service much the same thing?' Waite asked.

'Clearly, Waite, you haven't attended Military Academy – no fault of yours, of course,' he added smoothly as Waite bristled. 'You see, Military Intelligence seeks to acquire every piece of relevant military information on the enemy or potential enemies. Secret Service, on the other hand, involves espionage and counter-espionage. The first, simply stated, is finding out what are the enemy's secrets, plans and policies. The second is foiling them.'

'Then the Bolshevist threat is a serious one?'

'Oh, yes. Well, that is until Lenin dies. Then the whole rotten Bolshevist dictatorship will collapse with the inevitable in-fighting of that Red rabble. In the meantime, as the Reds are actively fomenting revolution among the working classes of Europe, the work of Section H is vital. So, notwithstanding your fluency in Russian, you'll need an apprenticeship of sorts. The Stepney Barracks instruction course commences in two day's time. That will prepare you, and work on the ground in Dublin will provide you with invaluable experience for when you take on the Bolshevists. Now, have you any questions?'

'No, Sir. Well, that is, not as regards the course. But as I have no bank account here yet, any cheque payments from my Simla bank's balance would be in rupees.'

'Don't worry about that, Waite. Scovel will give you a £10 float – for which you will sign – and that will carry you through until your new current account here is established. I shall also arrange permanent and more secure accommodation than your present hotel in Victoria.'

'Permanent accommodation, Maj ... Mr.Cromie?'

'For your later visits to London, that is. Far cheaper need I say than an hotel but, more importantly, a private place, namely The India Club. There, you'll be an Overseas Member. Your family and friends can maintain correspondence with you there.' He paused. 'You do have family, yes? Still in India?'

'Yes Sir.'

'By the way, the subject of cover names was dealt with in Cairo, I presume?'

'Oh, yes, Sir, it was.' Waite was pleased to be able to sound authoritative about something.

'And what name have you chosen?'

'Stephen Lexington.'

'Yes, that sounds O.K. Why did you choose that?'

'It was my grandmother's maiden name.'

'Good. You're not likely to forget it, then.'

'I think not, Sir.'

ooooo0000ooooo

Passing through the hotel's swing door, Kate approached the reception desk. 'Where is the sitting room, please?' she asked the young clerk. 'Just through the foyer to the left, Miss,' he replied, directing her to a door almost completely concealed by an enormous plant.

On her entrance, the room's only occupant rose. 'Miss Swanton?' he enquired.

'Yes,' she responded. 'And you are Mr Maguire?'

'I am indeed,' he replied. 'And let me say I am very pleased to see you. Do come and tell me how things went.' Taking her coat, he gestured towards one of the pair of leather wingback chairs in front of the fire. Placing her bag on the occasional table between them, she sat back and relaxed for the first time that day.

'I am very happy to tell you that the exercise was a complete success,' she said.

His stern features broke into a warm smile. 'I am greatly relieved, Miss Swanton. My congratulations. Please tell me all the details.'

Opening her bag, Kate removed the chamois purse and pushed it towards him. 'All thirty eight pounds exchanged for those sovereigns. And it all went without a hitch.'

'Excellent, excellent, Miss Swanton,' he exulted. 'Mr Collins will be delighted."

'However, the cashier in the final bank was a bit hesitant, so I used the first explanation and he was satisfied.'

'The Redhill one?'

'Yes.'

'Well, that is most encouraging. This means that we can go ahead with Mr Collins's plan to have selected Cumann na mBan women here in England follow in your footsteps.'

Kate frowned slightly. 'Mr Maguire, might I ask you ... why go to all this trouble when the sovereigns are of no more value than the one pound notes I exchanged for them?'

Maguire smiled. 'Simply stated, sovereigns have greater value abroad. For example, the market price in Aden recently was one pound seventeen shillings and sixpence for one full troy weight. That is a gross profit of about 75% as against its face value in London.'

Kate's eyes widened. 'That's an extraordinary level of profit!'

'Gold is the world's most precious metal,' Maguire said simply. 'It doesn't rust or tarnish and it is valued everywhere, as it is rarely found in commercial quantities.'

'So, to all intents and purposes, it is an alternative international currency,' Kate exclaimed. 'How ingenious.'

Maguire smiled, masking his surprise. He had not expected a young lady, especially such an attractive young lady, to have such insights.

'Let me offer you some refreshments,' he said, glancing around for the bell.

'Thank you, Mr Maguire, but I think I really should be on my way,' Kate responded. 'You see, I shall be returning to Dublin this evening and I have a few purchases to make before I leave.' Rising, she shook his hand.

21

'Perhaps we shall meet again in Dublin,' he smiled.

ooooo0OOO0ooooo

The Mail Boat

'Good morning, Madam. May I help you?'

Engrossed in her book, Kate had not noticed the steward
approach. Glancing at the menu, she ordered a poached egg
on toast and a pot of tea. Waiting, she glanced around the
dining saloon. Most of the diners were middle-aged men, one
a lone Army officer. To judge from the glint on his shoulder
tabs, he seemed of senior rank. Her gaze then fell on a young
man now at the entrance. Rather nice looking, and about her
own age, too. A steward led him towards her.

As they turned into an aisle, Waite saw a strikingly beautiful
young woman seated alone at a small table. He slowed his
pace. She looked up. Half-turning sideways the better to keep
her in view, Waite stumbled against a chair. Their eyes met.
Kate suppressed a smile. Now all she could see was his ramrod
straight back. Might he be a serving officer? She hoped not.

Waite sat at the table indicated, his mind's eye still holding the
image of her face. It took him a few moments to realise he was
staring with unseeing eyes at a monocled officer - a colonel no
less - at the table facing him. Restraining an involuntary salute,
he looked away.

22

'The menu, Sir. I'll be back for your order in a minute.'

Head down, he recalled her striking auburn hair, her creamy complexion, and her eyes. Especially her eyes. Were they green? He couldn't be certain. For a moment, he thought of going to her table and asking if he might share it with her. Unthinkable, of course. Waite was conscious of a feeling that he had never felt before. He longed to know this particular young lady, to be in her company.

Impulsively, he rose, almost colliding with the steward come to take his order, and sat at the opposite side of the table, where he would have a better view of her.

Kate, sipping her tea decorously, was completely aware of Waite's movements. He was staring at her. He was a rather handsome young man, she thought, as she buttered her toast. Once they were ashore, it might be impossible to meet him socially. How could she contrive to meet him ... accidentally? The germ of an idea struck.

Waite ate automatically, staring at her. Just then, she turned in his direction and their eyes met. His spirits soared as she held his gaze for a long moment, with – yes, the hint of a smile. In his imagination, he immediately saw them as ... well, companions. Might she have a preference for the theatre, concerts, art galleries? He was totally ignorant of musical entertainment – operetta? Gilbert and Sullivan? Although he had spent his school years in England, for him, London was a transit terminus – he was always either arriving at or leaving railway stations. There had been no time to spare then wandering about the West End, much less to visit theatres or the new picture houses.

She had beckoned a steward. Rising, she picked up her handbag and book and walked towards the entrance, not once looking in his direction. Crestfallen, he presumed that she was returning to her cabin. Would there ever be an opportunity to meet her again? He resolved to act now and somehow to strike up an acquaintance before they disembarked. He would go to his cabin for his bag and then linger on the passenger deck area until she came up on deck. Somehow he would contrive to strike up a conversation.

ooooo0000ooooo

'Jack, look!'

'Yeah, I see it.'

About 200 yards ahead a farmer's cart straddled the road, its horse grazing the verge. There was no sign of the driver. Disengaging the gears, Jack braked. About thirty yards or so from the cart, a flock of sheep scampered out of a field. In seconds they had blocked the road completely. Jack slowed the lorry to a stop.

'Right, Stan. Let's get this sorted. Leave your rifle on the seat, you won't need it to get those sheep back in the field.'

Just then, a Wicklow collie charged out of the gate, immediately followed by a farmhand who ineffectually attempted to round up the sheep. Stopping at the edge of the flock, Jack grinned at Stan's wariness. 'Don't worry, Stan, they don't bite and when they do it's only to eat grass.'

'Hands up!'

A man holding a gun and with a black scarf hiding his face came through the field's open gate. Several armed fellows followed – Volunteers they called themselves, Jack knew. Two held rifles, the rest an assortment of shotguns, all of them aimed at Jack and Stan. Both of them immediately raised their hands. The masked man, *Scarf* – as Jack mentally named him – shouted something in Irish. The Volunteers fanned out, two approaching the lorry.

'Where are your rifles?' *Scarf* snapped.

'Fuck off!' Jack attempted to sound as insolent as he could.

Scarf put the handgun to Stan's head and began counting. 'One, two....'

'Alright, there's only one rifle in the cab,' Jack said.

'Then go and get it now – and no tricks. There's more than one gun covering you.'

'Alright, I'm not stupid ...' Jack paused, knowing Stan was taking all this in, '... not like you lot with your guns pointing at a lorry full of petrol tins all ready for a stray bullet to blow up. I'll get the rifle.'

Returning, he held it upwards by the ice cold barrel and he handed it to one of the Volunteers.

Scarf gestured with his gun. 'Get in the lorry now and turn it around.'

'Drive it yourself!' Jack retorted.

Scarf turned to Stan.

'Can you drive this lorry?'

Jack saw the relief on Stan's face as he shook his head.

'What's your name, Soldier?'

'Pinkston, Sir. Private, No. 319 ...'

'Never mind that. What's your first name?'

'Stanley, Sir.'

Scarf turned to Jack.

'Now, Mr. Smart Alec, what's your first name?'

'Jack.'

'Well, Jack, if you don't get behind the wheel of that fucking lorry and drive it, Stanley here will have his brains blown out. And if you don't follow any other orders I give you, you'll end up with a bullet in the head beside him.'

Jack's assent held as much muted defiance as he could muster. 'Am I supposed to drive through the sheep?'

'Joe, get that farmhand and his dog out here,' *Scarf* shouted without turning his head. 'And you, Seamus, get that horse and cart back in the field once the sheep are off the road.'

When the road was clear, Jack reversed the lorry halfway into the field and then drove it out to face back the way he had just come. *Scarf*, gun in hand, swung himself up beside him in the passenger seat.

'What about Stan?' Jack said.

'Don't worry about him. He'll be looked after until we're finished with the petroleum and the lorry.'

Jack concentrated on his driving. About four miles further on *Scarf* spoke. 'Next left.'

Jack swung the lorry into a boreen with a rough uneven surface and potholes.

'Well, I won't be needing this for now.' *Scarf* pushed his gun into the pocket of his trench coat. Driving more slowly, Jack gave way now and again to farmers' carts, driven livestock and stray sheep. O'Reilly had assured him that nothing would happen once they were well away from the main roads. To come on a military patrol now would be a rare thing. And though the RIC still had foot patrols few, if any, ventured into the wider countryside without military support. By now, most of the smaller police barracks and outpost huts in the remote areas lay abandoned, if not burnt down by the Shinners. The Peelers no longer had complete run of much of the Irish countryside.

'You handled yourself well back there, Jack. Very convincing.'

Jack glanced sideways. *Scarf* had uncovered his face. Jack had never seen him before.

'Will the tins be going to Birr?' he ventured.

'Who would buy tins of petroleum in Birr, Jack? The one big shop-owner there has only the one delivery lorry. It would take him more than a year to use up all the fuel that's behind us. And the rest of the small traders still use horse vans or carts for local deliveries. Hay and oats are still cheaper than petroleum. And as for selling it to the gentry, most of them are probably shareholders in the Anglo-Persian Oil Company. So buying stolen petrol would be robbing themselves.'

'Wouldn't Limerick city be big enough to have enough buyers?'

'Exactly. That's where it'll be going.'

'Will I be driving it there?'

'Of course not, Jack. The petrol will be sent there in milk churns while the military and police are still searching for this lorry.' He paused. 'Now, there's a turn somewhere along the next quarter mile. We're to keep a look out for a willow tree on the left. That'll be close to it.'

As he drove, Jack reflected on how much convincing it had taken to persuade O'Reilly that stolen British army petroleum could be a handy source of money for his Irish Volunteers.

ooooo0000ooooo

Two hours later, Jack was on the Dublin train from Limerick, sharing a compartment with three countrymen – comfortable farmers by the look of them. Avoiding conversation, he closed his eyes on taking his seat. A little over an hour later, the third and last of his fellow-travellers got off at the railway station in Portarlington. With the compartment to himself, he opened his leather case and pulled out a copy of the *Irish Field*. He liked a flutter on the nags and had learned early on that doing

28

accumulator betting was the best way to gamble. You bet a small sum on one horse and if it won your winnings then went on your second horse and so on. Though Percy had taught him how to do accumulators, Jack never spent more than one penny on any bet. That wasn't much of a wager to lose if any of the four, five or six horses you had picked in different races failed to pass the winning post. Percy threw his money around and made up for any losses with some discreet robbing. Jack grinned. Whatever was that chancer up to now? A fella as slippery as him could be up to anything.

The screech of the train's whistle brought him back to the present. Glancing at his wrist-watch he figured it would be well over an hour before reaching Dublin. With no danger of interruption he would check exactly how much he was worth. Pulling up the left leg of his trousers to knee level he exposed a bandage covering it from knee to ankle. Undoing the large safety pin securing that, he unwound it carefully until the edge of a flattened wad of bank notes appeared. Yeah, the six five pound, three one pound and the single ten shilling notes were all there. It took several minutes for him to put them all back securely in place. He knew that he had saved more than enough to get him to the United States when it suited him, and plenty to live on there until he figured out what to do with his life. But for now he'd go along with this Volunteer business. It was getting interesting. Settling back into the corner of the seat, he closed his eyes.

The jolting of the carriage woke him as the train approached Kingsbridge Station. Following the other passengers along the platform, he joined the queue for one of the horse cabs waiting alongside the station. He directed the jarvey to take him to Vaughan's Hotel in Parnell Square.

Progress was slow along the north quays of the Liffey. He knew they had turned into Sackville Street when he spotted Nelson's Pillar in the middle of the street ahead. Passing the front of a large pillared building he recognised it from newspaper photographs as the former General Post Office. It had been the headquarters of the 1916 rebels until artillery shells made a ruin of it. A little later, the cabbie shouted back. 'I'll be stopping at Vaughan's Hotel in a few seconds, Sir.'

Jack looked up at the hotel as he alighted. Like the others on the square, it was a large red-brick three-storey building. Climbing the few steps up to the entrance he stepped into the small space between the front door and the glass-panelled inner door. An elderly porter responded to his knock.

'Good day, Sir.'

'And a good day to you too,' Jack smiled. 'Are there any vacancies, please? I'd like to stay a couple of nights.'

'Certainly, Sir. Come in and I'll book you in.'

Following him down the long hallway, they stopped at a table with the Visitors' Book.

'You have to sign this, Sir, before I can let you have a room key. You see, the Peel... the Constabulary do sometimes come in at night after hours to check that people drinking here are proper residents. They're checkin' it's not a *shebeen.*'

Mention of the Peelers definitely meant that he couldn't use the name Dougherty anymore. So think fast for another. 'So where do I sign?'

'Just there, Sir.'

Jack hesitated – what name would he use now? Kelly? Yes. Thousands of Kelly's around. He signed the register.

'And your occupation, Sir?'

Jack wrote *Commercial Traveller.*

'How long will you be staying with us, Sir?'

'Oh, I'll be here just a few days.'

'You've come from Limerick, haven't you, Sir?'

Shocked, Jack hesitated before replying easily. 'You must be a mind reader.'

'No, I'm not that, Sir. It's just that Mr. Price – a businessman – asked me to let him know when the traveller from Limerick got here.'

Not yet an hour in Dublin and the Shinners were already calling on him, Jack thought grimly as he followed the porter to his room. Twenty minutes later, as he mopped his face, he heard tapping on his door. Tense, he reached under the pillow for his gun.

'Who is it?

'It's me, Sir, the porter. That Mr. Price is here to see you.'

ooooo0000ooooo

31

Royal Marine Hotel, Kingstown, Co. Dublin

Collins strode into the lounge and approached the saturnine figure of Sam Maguire, seated on a leather couch.

'Can I pour you a cup?' Sam enquired, holding the coffee pot.

'Please,' Collins replied. 'I gather that the trial run by the Swanton girl seems to have worked out alright?'

'One fine day doesn't make a summer, Mick,' Sam responded. 'We can have the selected Cumann na mBan women take over there, as planned, but they will have to be instructed on how and what precisely they are to do – Miss Swanton would be useful there. There is also the list to be drawn up of all the bank branches to be visited and a timetable for each of them. And as we can't have the same woman revisit any one bank for at least five or six weeks, that will involve precise planning. The second visit...'

'OK, I see what you're getting at, Sam,' Collins interjected. 'At this rate, it will take time. In the meantime, there's a fair bit of cash mixed in with business and professional accounts around Ireland – not to say a few Parish Church accounts here and there - that is not earning a penny interest. More to the point,' he went on 'there's a Police Magistrate by the name of Bell who is sniffing around looking for this Dáil money.'

Sam frowned. 'If he uses the 1880s Coercion Act, he'll find every penny in every bank.'

'Well, we'll have to sort that,' Collins lit a cigarette.

'Will you need anyone from the organisation in London to help?'

'For the Bell job, no, we can do that here. Anything else on your mind, Sam?'

'What's the news from America?'

Collins smiled. 'Dev has sent about $200,000 so far and $100,000 of that has gone to London, care of Art O'Brien. Bob Briscoe is over in Hamburg taking delivery of 300 rifles. Art will arrange to forward the balance of the price from a City firm in London.'

'Art is doing a damn good job,' Sam said. 'I haven't heard a whisper about that business from my Scotland House contacts. In fact, the only problem I see now is that I get all your copy wires on matters concerning the Firm, but they are a bit late in coming. We're having decoding delays in London because of the increase in wires from America.'

Collins stubbed out his cigarette. 'I'm having the same problem in Dublin with wires coming in from Head Centres all over the British Empire. I've been able to have some extra men trained by a couple of our Post Office telegraphists here in Dublin, but we do need more.'

They lapsed into silence.

'By the way, Mick,' Sam said, 'did you know that there is no such thing as a Police Magistrate anywhere in England, Scotland and Wales?'

Collins regarded him quizzically. 'No, I didn't. And you're going to tell me why.'

'Because there are no rebels in England, Scotland or Wales.'

Collins grinned. 'And what about the Suffragettes?'

ooooo0000ooooo

'Will I carry your bags up to the gangway, Ma'am?'

Kate, her eyes fixed on the stairs to the men's saloon below, had not noticed the steward's approach.

'Not yet, thank you.'

'Excuse me, please.'

Kate made way for a woman passing. Just then she saw the young man from the dining room come into view where the stairway turned upwards. He was behind a slow-moving elderly man. Bending, Kate grasped her handbag and valise in one hand and her portmanteau in the other. Inching forward, she moved towards the steps. In seconds, a voice behind her spoke. 'May I be of assistance, Miss?' It was the young man.

'Oh, that would be most kind of you, thank you.' She smiled up at him. 'It is all rather a crush, don't you think?'

Waite seized the moment. 'Why don't you stand aside for a few minutes and allow the crowd to pass, while I take your bags up to the gangway? The steward there could keep an eye on them until we follow.' Kate hesitated. 'And in the meantime, you could look after my bag?'

'That is a good idea, Mr...?'

'Oh, Lexington,' Waite said. 'Stephen Lexington.' Waite felt a complete cad. For the first time in his life he has the chance, the slimmest of slim chances of making the acquaintance of a beautiful and captivating young woman, and he begins with a

34

lie.

'My name is Katherine Swanton,' she replied.

Realising that he was beaming at her longer than was called for, Waite grasped both her bags. His eyes widened when he felt the weight of her portmanteau.

'Books, I'm afraid, Mr Lexington,' Kate smiled. 'It's rather heavy, isn't it.'

'Not at all, Miss Swanton,' Waite breathed in and braced himself. 'You really did need a steward, didn't you! Back in a jiffy.'

Watching him struggle up the stairway, Kate felt genuine contrition for telling him a pack of lies. Had the portmanteau not been locked, she would not have parted with it. Inside were the current *Army List*, the latest editions of *Who's Who*, *Kelly's London Street Directory*, *Burke's Peerage* and *Dod's Parliamentary Companion*. She would certainly have some explaining to do if Mr Lexington became aware of what he was labouring to carry. Nevertheless, their being required by a solicitor's firm was not entirely implausible. *Burke's Peerage* and the *Army List* were useful reference sources. Prudent business owners would have their solicitors check *Kelly's* to validate the existence of firms that commercial travellers purported to represent. However, she reflected, explaining the legal or commercial need to hold a copy of *Dod's* would be a challenge. Mr Lexington was unlikely to know that all elected Sinn Féin Members of Parliament were pledged not to take their seats at Westminster, and that *Dod's* also had the home addresses of all MPs and Peers, some of whom would be on the mailing list of the *Irish Bulletin*.

Once on deck, Waite approached the steward on gangway duty and placed the bags beside him. 'Could you keep an eye on these, please?' he asked. 'I'll just pick up a few more. I'll be right back.'

'That'll be grand, sir. I'll be here for the next hour, so take your time.'

Kate was standing where he had left her. 'The steward chap with whom I spoke said he would have a deckhand carry your weekend case safely down the gangway.'

'How very thoughtful of you, Mr Lexington.' Kate smiled.

'It is really quite weighty. I can't imagine how you would have managed with it,' Waite said.

'It is indeed,' Kate agreed. 'You see, law books and commercial directories are a necessary reference source for legal practitioners like my employer. As it is cheaper to purchase them in London, it made sense for me to do so as I visit there quite frequently.'

They climbed the steps to the deck. 'Your bags are down there, Sir,' the steward pointed to where they had been placed, out of the way of the passengers. 'Thank you, Sir,' as Waite passed him a few coins.

When they stood on the quayside, Kate turned to Waite. 'You've been very kind, Mr Lexington, thank you very much. I shan't be taking the train from here as my destination is closer and a cab will suit.'

Flustered, Waite stammered 'Let me at least carry your weekend case to the cab rank.' He signalled to the deckhand to follow them with Kate's cases. 'I have to wait for my trunk, so I am in no hurry.'

Walking along the station platform together, Kate broke the awkward silence. 'Is this your first time in Ireland, Mr Lexington?'

'Oh yes, indeed.'

'You are hardly a tourist?' she enquired.

'Alas, no. I am taking up the position of insurance agent here for the Home and Colonial Insurance Company – everybody calls it the H&C. Perhaps you have heard of it?'

'I'm afraid not. But then there are so many insurance firms,' she said.

'I am beginning to realise that now, Miss Swanton. Our company is a little different, as it covers business and commercial property. Most of the others are better known because they cover life and home insurance. And ... ah, we're here.' Waite opened the half door of a waiting horse carriage. Lifting her valise, he pushed it across the cab's floor as the cabman heaved her portmanteau on board.

Kate turned to him and offered her hand. 'You have been most helpful, Mr Lexington. Thank you.'

'It was my pleasure, Miss Swanton,' he shook her hand vigorously and then dropped it, in case he might have hurt her.

Kate climbed into the cab. 'Oh, just one thing,' Waite called. He fumbled in his pocket book and drew out a business calling card. 'It has only my firm's London address at present. But as soon as I am settled I will be provided with new cards. That is, em, in case you... or rather, your firm ... would be interested ... an estimate, something like that?'

Kate took the card. 'What a good idea,' she said. 'I must mention it to my employer. Perhaps you would be good enough to push the door shut – it's easier to do that from the outside. And thank you again, Mr Lexington.'

As the cab moved slowly away, Waite walked alongside for a few paces. Kate turned, smiled warmly and was gone.

ooooo0000ooooo

An annex to the War Office, Whitehall, London, January 1920

'Major Anderson is here, Colonel.'

'Show him in, Captain.' Putting aside the papers on his desk, the Colonel looked up as his visitor, a man of middle years about his own age, entered. 'Good morning, Albert,' he smiled, motioning him to a chair.

'Morning, Clive,' Albert settled himself, 'I must say your telephone call yesterday was rather vague, what?'

'Of necessity, yes,' Clive responded. 'Sir Henry has enjoined me to strictest secrecy in this matter and, as of this minute, this applies to you.'

'Ah, let me guess,' his visitor grinned. 'Thomson's sleuths have uncovered yet another Bolshevist conspiracy to suborn serving soldiers, yes?'

'Let us be thankful that Sir Basil has not yet found anything of the sort,' Clive said drily. 'But, yes, it is a conspiracy of sorts that threatens disaffection in the lower ranks of the Army.'

'Ah,' Albert said cheerily. 'That would be the Bolshevists' intrigues with the trade unions, yes?'

Clive stared. 'How on earth do you know about that?'

'If you would only get out of the office now and again, Clive, and visit your Club more often, you would know that that is the most repetitive refrain among members, apart from the lamentations about securing reliable servants.'

Clive looked severe. 'You are being frivolous, Albert. This is a serious matter. Sir Basil has informed the Cabinet that Bolshevist schemers from Moscow are here in London, posing as diplomats, and are secretly funding *The Daily Worker*. And they have also infiltrated the trade unions with agitators, particularly the railwaymen and dock workers.'

'With respect, Clive,' Albert said, 'Basil's penny dreadful weekly does go overboard with its alarmist conspiracy theories...'

'How to you know about the *Pink Paper*, Albert?' Clive asked sharply. 'I haven't seen your name on the authorised address list.'

'Indeed no, it is not,' Albert said soothingly. 'With the War now in the past, when old friends gather in their Clubs, they do share confidences, you know.'

Clive relaxed. 'You must bear in mind that, as head of the Special Branch, Sir Basil has a myriad of country-wide sources that keep him informed of all current contacts between the trade unions and the Bolshevists. It is a literal fact that Bolshevist gold – gold, no less – is financing not only *The Daily Worker* but also the printing of incendiary pamphlets, aimed at inciting the working classes to revolution. Have you forgotten the disgraceful spectacle of serving British soldiers virtually laying siege to Downing Street?' he demanded.

'That was a year ago, Clive, and Army demobilisation had hardly begun. Hardly surprising that disaffected soldiers without a job to go to became a little hotheaded. Mind you, the sight of them milling outside No. 10 must have put the wind up the PM,' he reflected.

'And not just the PM, Albert,' Clive said severely. 'Sir Henry was apoplectic after making his way through them on his way into No. 10. All of them knew full well that he was their Chief, yet not one single man saluted!'

'Why didn't he command them to disperse and return to barracks,' Albert asked, interested.

'I didn't attain this position, Albert, by questioning a superior officer's decision,' Clive snapped.

'Or his indecision...'

'Really, Albert, you can be most indiscreet at times and usually at the wrong time. I will concede – privately – that in the main you are well-intentioned. However,' he looked meaningfully at his guest, 'you wouldn't be in this office today had we not been pals since school. It's all your own doing that you remain a major with only, what, four years to retirement?'

'That, Clive, I happily acknowledge,' Albert beamed. 'Indeed, I would have been despatched from the Army long ago were it not for your good offices. Believe me to be truly grateful.'

Clive sighed. 'Let's get down to business, Albert. There is a matter which greatly vexes Sir Henry and that is why I have asked you here today.'

Albert looked intrigued.

'There is the potential for a major scandal – if it is revealed – of corruption in the Army,' Clive said portentously. 'I want you to investigate it as discreetly as possible.'

'Corruption?'

'Yes. The widespread and flagrant larceny of Army property, particularly that of petroleum.'

ooooo0000ooooo

25 March 1920

'£997... £998 ...£999 ... and there, the final £1, giving us a grand total of £1,000.' The elderly bank manager looked enquiringly at Kate. She nodded. Mr Keogh's rapid-fire counting of bank notes was always accurate.

'You know, Miss Swanton, £1,000 these days would buy a substantial house in Ballsbridge. Bearing such a large sum of money in Dublin these days is not to be recommended to businessmen, let alone to young ladies.'

Regarding her with genuine concern, he signed inwardly, wishing he were a young man again.

'I have been doing this for some months now,' Kate informed him with some asperity.

'You have,' he agreed.

'And who would suspect a lady of carrying such a sum through the streets of Dublin? That is what safeguards the money, Mr Keogh.' Not to mention, unbeknownst to Mr Keogh, the armed Volunteer walking a few paces behind her.

'Indeed, Miss Swanton, indeed.'

'And do remember that two weeks ago I lodged a negotiable Bill of Exchange very many times the value of this withdrawal,' she said.

'Yes, Miss Swanton, I do remember that.' It had been a gratifyingly large lodgement for the client account of Pigot, La Touche and O'Brien, drawn on the account of the Malayan Tea Company Ltd. at the London branch of the Shanghai and Peking Bank Limited in favour of, and duly endorsed by, Mr Robert Briscoe, Commercial Agent, Dublin. Mr Keogh divided the £1,000 pounds before him into compact wads of one hundred pound notes kept together with elastic bands. He frowned, his concern for her persisting. Every month since October, she had cashed a cheque for £1,000, drawn on her firm's client's account. Large withdrawals from deposit accounts, although inevitable, were not exactly welcomed by bank managers. However, he had noted with satisfaction, and some curiosity, the recent substantial increase of transfers of cash deposits among and between other solicitors and business firms. Additional cash deposits were always gratifying. Kate's

42

polite cough broke his reverie.

'Goodness, Miss Swanton, I almost forgot. You should be aware of a rather disturbing official document which I received yesterday.' Removing a foolscap sheet of parchment from a drawer, he laid it on the desk.

'As an apprentice solicitor, legal assistant and Mr O'Brien's niece, you would, I feel certain, have a greater interest and concern for the practice than an ordinary clerk.'

'But of course, Mr Keogh.' What on earth was he talking about?

'I have here - in common, I believe with other bank managers – a formal communication from the authorities in Dublin Castle. This,' he announced, lifting up the parchment with a flourish, 'is a Summons!'

It was probably, Kate reflected, the first ever summons served on him in all of his respectable life. She knew exactly what it was about. The newspapers had already reported the establishment of Mr Bell's tribunal and its opening next week in the Castle. Suppressing a smile, she looked attentive.

'Why not read it yourself, Miss Swanton, while I go to have my secretary fetch a stout manila envelope.' Rising, he passed the Summons across the desk.

'Whereas the following bodies Sinn Féin, the Irish Republican Brotherhood, Oglaigh na hÉireann or the Irish Volunteers, Dáil Éireann etc. have been proclaimed illegal organisations by the Lieutenant and General Governor of Ireland, Field Marshall Sir John French. THIS IS TO COMMAND YOU to appear as witness before me at the Police Court, Inn's Quay,

Dublin on the 31st day of March, 1920, at 11 o'clock a.m. then and there to be examined before me, touching the premises, and to bring with you and produce for examination Securities, Telegrams, Copies of Telegrams, Letters, Copies of Letters, all books of Accounts, Ledgers, Vouchers, Bills, Cheques, Orders or drafts, Records, Memoranda and other documents in any way relating to any dealings or transactions between your Bank and the said organisations or any of them, or any committee or body constituted by or acting in privity with them, or any of them, which are now in your power, possession or procurement, or in the power, possession or procurement of your Bank.

Dated at the Police Courts, Inn's Quay, Dublin this Saturday, 20th day of March 1920.

Signed,   ALAN BELL Resident Magistrate

for the County of Dublin, duly qualified according to Law.

Replacing the Summons on the desk, Kate sat back. The Dublin Castle authorities were determined to get their hands on the Dáil Éireann National Loan Fund. Their first attempt had been in January, when police and military raided the Sinn Féin Bank in Harcourt Street. The modest cash balances they seized had to be returned as they were found to belong to legitimate, irate, depositors. Although not a penny of the Loan Fund money was found there, the bank was subsequently closed down. The draconian powers of the 1882 Coercion Act were then invoked to allow Mr Bell's 'Star Chamber' to replace the courts. Kate marvelled at the authorities' naiveté in believing that either Dáil Éireann or the clandestine Irish Volunteers would have bank accounts in their own names. Sinn Féin, until now an open political party would, of course, have an impeccable set of accounts.

Kate's maternal grandfather, an Old Fenian and a stalwart of the ultra-secret Irish Republican Brotherhood, had enthralled his little granddaughter with stirring tales of Irish history. In her teenage years, she had come to realise that her grandfather had been somehow involved in the fight for freedom, as indeed had her uncle, in whose solicitor's practice she now worked. She had a reasonably good understanding of the IRB's structure and its methods of operation, though she couldn't know who was on its Supreme Council or who was or was not a member. That said, she had a shrewd idea who was its Head Centre, as Grandpapa termed the top man's title. Although it seemed to be a men-only body, someone had once mentioned that Madam Maud Gonne MacBride was a member. Well, if female membership was permitted, Kate reflected, she hadn't been invited to join – so far, anyway.

The Castle's efforts to lay hands on any Dáil, Volunteer or IRB funds had been futile. They had long been dispersed in banks throughout Ireland and, to a lesser extent, in England. Kate suspected that Sinn Féin money was probably mingled in composite accounts with the unlawful gains of tax evasion by so-called pillars of Irish society. No matter the beneficial owner, no bank manager could possibly identify the owners of such concealed monies. And that, she reflected, meant that Mr Bell would have to subpoena every solicitor in Ireland for each client file. Should he attempt that, the solicitors' representative body would be up in arms with a test case. And that, wending its way all through the lower courts to the Law Lords in London, would mean further delay for Mr Bell's investigation.

The door opened and Mr Keogh bustled into the room bearing the sealing wax stick. Five minutes more fussing saw

45

the manila envelope containing the neatly packed wads of pound notes gummed, sealed with the bank's stamp, and securely in Kate's possession. Once in the bank's public area, she walked to one of the side tables. Placing the envelope on the blotting pad, she took a pen from the stand and dipped it into the inkwell. In her best copperplate hand, she wrote the addressee's details. She turned the envelope over and pressed it down on the blotting pad. If any Castle spy were hanging around and took it into his head to check, the mirror image of the lines she had written would be on the blotter. His Grace, Dr Michael Walsh, Catholic Archbishop of Dublin had no inkling that his name appeared so frequently on such envelopes. Efficiently, Kate stuck the required postage stamps on the envelope, in the sure knowledge that this, like all its predecessors, would never reach the inside of a Post Office. The Dáil Minister for Finance, Mr Collins, was the intended recipient.

Chapter 2

'If England goes on like this she will lose the Empire. There is
absolutely no grip anywhere. I propose, after the New Year ...
to take a rather active part in matters - even in some (like
Ireland and Egypt) which are not solely military.'

Field Marshal Sir Henry Wilson, Chief of the Imperial General
Staff

Diaries, 30 November, 1919

Dalkey tram to Dublin, 9.15 a.m., 25 March 1920

'Fares, please.'

Jack had boarded the tram at Dalkey, a small village on the southern outskirts of Dublin. A couple of women and two elderly men took their seats on the lower deck well away from the draughty open platform, so Jack had the bench seat there to himself. He had an almost complete view of the platform as well as of the narrow winding stairs to the open upper deck where smokers, the young and the hardy chose to sit. Unfolding his copy of the *Morning Post*, he laid it on his lap, checking that the butt of the .38 automatic was within easy reach in his inside pocket.

As the tram gradually lost speed approaching the Monkstown stop, the conductor remained on the upper deck collecting fares. The tram stopped. As the trellis half-gate on the platform was drawn back, Jack raised his *Morning Post* to eye level. A single passenger boarded. A quick glance through the side window confirmed it was Bell, the Police Magistrate. As the tram moved off slowly he glanced back. Bell's detective escort was walking away in the opposite direction to take up his post outside the magistrate's house. Bell sat on the bench seat opposite Jack and blew his nose into a large handkerchief.

Hearing the rustle of the old man's newspaper, Jack slowly lowered his *Post*. All he could see of Bell was the brim of his black bowler hat and the lower part of his buttoned black overcoat, black trousers and highly polished boots. He looked every bit the gent as when he had been pointed out to Jack the previous week in Dame Street. Though he could easily pass for a lawyer or a banker, Mr Alan Bell was a Police Magistrate. They, Jack had been told, were only to be found in Ireland. Almost all magistrates had started out as Peelers and then risen up the ranks to the level of Inspector in the R.I.C. or the Dublin Metropolitan Police. Some were former Army officers. Police Magistrates had a reputation for giving little quarter to criminals and none at all to active Nationalists. Many of them – including Bell, he had been told, wore Wilkinson bullet-proof body armour under their shirts. And all of them most certainly carried the short-barrel RIC five chamber .45 pocket revolver. That, Jack knew, packed almost the same punch at close range as its Webley big brother. But for all that, Jack's .38 was just as deadly. Yeah, he reflected, this Bell fella must be causing a lot of trouble to the high-ups in the Volunteers if they wanted him plugged.

ooooo0000ooooo

Waite was inexplicably nervous as he made his sales pitch to the Dublin businessman. It was ironic, he reflected, that he was more ill-at-ease in his new role as insurance salesman than he had ever been as a soldier.

'Well now, Mr Lexington, I cannot give you a decision today. That said, your quotation for damage to property arising from riot, civil unrest and so on is very keen, and I shall discuss it with my fellow directors.'

'Perhaps, Mr. McKeever, when you do discuss it with them, you might also stress that the big advantage of the Home and Colonial Insurance Company is in the spread of its insurance activities throughout the Empire. It has greater resources than a locally based insurer to back up major claims.'

'That is a good point, Mr. Lexington, and I shall certainly bear it in mind. However...' he paused. Waite's rising elation stalled. '...given the lawless state of affairs in Ireland, it seems very courageous of you to be promoting a British Company's business here.'

'Not really, Sir. I was in far greater danger throughout the War,' Waite said carefully.

'Yes, that is indeed true.'

'And besides, as a former officer in civilian attire, I am no different, surely, than thousands of men in both of our islands?'

'Well, no, perhaps not.'

McKeever stared out of the window. After a few moments, he turned back. 'Have you lost any relatives or friends in the War, Mr Lexington?'

'No, Mr. McKeever. You see, I have no brothers or male cousins. That said, and with the passage of time, I have learned that a number of my school chums did not survive the War.'

'Our only son fell at Ypres, a cadet officer of just 20 years of age.'

Waite was lost for words. It was his first encounter with a bereaved parent. He nodded in respectful sympathy, 'I'm very sorry to learn of that, sir,' he said.

'Thank you, Mr. Lexington.'

In the silence that followed, it struck Waite that this man's son was probably the same age as himself. And perhaps he reminded this grieving man in some way of his dead boy.

'Well, the War is over now and life must go on, Mr Lexington.' McKeever spoke in a forced lighter tone. 'Or so we thought until the Shinners brought murder back to the streets of Dublin.'

Alert, Waite recalled his Stepney instructor's words: *watch out for the comment or remark that shows where their loyalty lies.*

'This is my first time in Dublin, Mr. McKeever,' he said carefully, 'but from what I have read in the newspapers, it seems that most of the disturbances are in the country areas. I have only been here one day, but it seems a very normal city to me.'

'Dublin may seem a normal city, Mr. Lexington, but let me tell you there are respectably dressed young thugs walking the streets here. In London, they would pass as decent fellows. But here they have innocent faces, guns in their pockets and murder in their hearts.'

'Really?'

'Oh yes and, worse, the authorities seem to lack the resolution to pursue them.'

'Is there not a criminal detection department in the Dublin Police?' Waite was intrigued.

'There is – or rather there was until recently. And I understand – and please do not repeat this – that their best detectives have all been shot dead. The remaining ones are too intimidated to investigate the proscribed organisations. Indeed, I believe their usual informants now avoid them.'

This tallied with what Cromie had said was the state of affairs in Ireland.

'Furthermore, many Roman Catholic businessmen of my acquaintance have told me in confidence that they regarded their contribution to the so-called Dáil Éireann Loan as just a form of insurance to protect their property – their businesses.'

Waite saw an opening at last. 'Mr. McKeever, may I tell you something that may be of interest to you?'

'By all means, Mr. Lexington.'

'There is a section of special insurance inspectors at the Head Office of the Home and Colonial in London. These gentlemen, I understand, spend their time constantly examining potential risks in all overseas countries in which the company carries on business.'

'Potential risks? Of what kind?'

'Risks arising from political or economic turmoil.'

'Such as what obtains now in Ireland?'

'Yes, indeed it does, Mr. McKeever, and so, thanks to these gentlemen, I can confidentially tell you that the Home and Colonial will shortly have an additional insurance policy which will supplement the shortfall of a court award for a claim under last year's Malicious Damage, Death and Injury Act. That, as I am sure you know, applied solely to Ireland. Now that is to be welcomed, isn't it?'

'Oh, yes, of course.' McKeever said.

'I must emphasise that it is a highly confidential policy matter of the firm.' Waite added. 'If it became publicly known, the present court awards under the Malicious Damages Act may well drop in value.'

McKeever paused for a few moments. 'These special insurance inspector fellows you speak of seem to think of everything.'

'Yes, indeed. For that reason, having as much information as possible about what is going on everywhere the H&C does business is vitally important.' Waite paused. 'For instance, should you learn of anything that would better inform those gentlemen of the state of affairs in Dublin and Ireland, that is, of matters not otherwise available from the newspapers, such information might well be most helpful.' He waited.

McKeever stared at the surface of the desk.

'So what do you think, Mr. McKeever?'

McKeever squared his shoulders. 'I should be most agreeable to assist those gentlemen, Mr. Lexington, should the opportunity arise.'

'Then ... oh, I do apologise. You haven't finished.'

'Thank you. I was going to say I would have two reservations. Firstly, those gentlemen in London may well be alarmed at the underlying political instability here and increase premiums for Irish policies.'

'I can assure you, Mr. McKeever, your premium would not be increased. Indeed there might well be a percentage rebate of your premium for ... em ... really useful information.'

'I understand you, Mr Lexington. However, given the thefts by gunmen here of Post Office mail bags, I would be very reluctant to put my name to any information sent to you.'

'Have no concern about that detail, Mr. McKeever. There will be no need for you ever to identify yourself in any way. I shall give you an address in London to which you can – anonymously – post on any such information that comes your way. That is, of course, if you are so minded?'

'Indeed I am, Mr. Lexington. Do please tell me more.'

Waite was jubilant.

ooooo0OOOOooooo

Bell continued to read his *Irish Times*, his usual habit, Jack had been told. Jack's instructions were to watch out in case a policeman boarded the tram and sat beside the magistrate. In that case, Jack was to get off the tram at Ailesbury Road and the Volunteers waiting there would know that the job was off. Bell sneezed again. Jack couldn't make out why he sat at the draughty end of the bench seat, the one that got the full blast of any gale that was going. Then, at each stop, he observed Bell lower his newspaper and size up the passengers coming onto the tram. 'Well, once a Peeler always a Peeler,' he reflected.

At Ailesbury Road, nine well-dressed young men boarded. Six of them climbed the stairs to the upper deck. Three passed Jack and took separate seats on the lower deck. As the tram moved off, Jack prepared for the next stop ahead – the one that really mattered – outside the Royal Dublin Society grounds at Ballsbridge. Heavy footsteps on the stairway interrupted Bell's reading. Two of the men who had just ascended to the upper deck returned to the platform. Turning a page, Jack glanced sideways. They stood facing outwards with their hands on the safety rails. One of the Volunteers took the few paces to the conductor's alcove under the winding metal stairs and pressed the button there, signalling the driver to halt at the next stop. He rejoined his companion. As the tram gradually lost speed, Jack heard the Volunteers drawing back the trellis gate. Bell was again absorbed in his *Irish Times*. The driver had cut off power to the motor and the tram lumbered forward, gradually slowing down. Yards from the stop, he gave the brake-wheel a few rapid turns and the tram trundled to a smooth halt. There was no-one waiting. Bell glanced up briefly and returned to his paper. The conductor was on the upper deck collecting fares. The Volunteers on the platform stepped down on to the cobbles and chatted as they waited to cross the road.

The conductor started down the stairs to close the trellis gate before signalling the driver to move off. By now, Jack knew the Volunteers remaining on the upper deck would have pulled down the lanyard of the trolley pole and dragged it sideways. As its small wheel lost contact with the high voltage street cable, the tram's electric motor stopped. Jack tensed, ready to use the .38 if it became necessary. Two of the Volunteers on the lower deck rose and approached Bell. 'Are you Mr. Bell?' one of the young men barked. Lowering his paper in surprise, he glared at them.

'I am, but who....?'

'Your time has come, Mr. Bell!'

The words were hardly spoken before the two grabbed hold of his arms and dragged him from his seat on to the platform. Until then, outrage and shock had slowed the old man's reaction. The conductor froze, appalled. Jack stood. Along with some of other passengers he watched Bell grasping the platform handrail with both hands as his captors sought to drag him from the tram. The last two Volunteers now clattered down the stairs and joined the others in manhandling him. Bell's grip was broken. Dragging him onto the roadway, they hauled him across the cobbles, knocking off his hat in the melee. Close to the kerb, they released him, stepping back a few paces. Bell, shocked and confused, staggered, trying to regain his balance. Moving closer, one of his attackers aimed a gun at the Magistrate's head. As he fired, Bell jerked his head sideways. The bullet sped harmlessly by. As his killer re-aimed for a second head shot, Bell thrust out his hand, deflecting the pistol downwards as it fired. The bullet penetrated his groin. Bell recoiled and half-turned his head. The final bullet struck him behind the ear. Lifeless, he fell backwards, his body straddling the road and granite kerb. A lady passenger screamed and fainted. In panic, the conductor scrambled up the stairs to the upper deck and pleaded with the passengers there to do something. Bell's killer stooped down and looked closely at the fatal head wound. Tapping the dying man's chest with his pistol, he straightened up and nodded to his accomplices. Mick had been right – as usual. Bell wore body armour. Nothing but a head shot would have done this job. His killers turned and calmly walked their separate ways from the macabre scene – secure in the knowledge that no-one would dare to follow as they dispersed in the quiet, tree-lined avenues of Dublin's most fashionable suburb. By now, Jack had joined the few curious passengers – all male – who had gathered around the dead Magistrate. A few seconds later he turned away and walked towards the city centre. Time, he decided, to move on before the Peelers arrived. Crossing the main road, he turned the corner into Serpentine Road as instructed. In a little over five minutes he reached Sandymount Green. He knocked twice on the side door of the green-painted pub there and was admitted. He handed over the .38 to the barman, left and walked the short distance to catch a tram at Ringsend for the city centre.

ooooo0000oooooo

Whitehall

A perfunctory tap at the door was followed in short order by Albert's beaming face as he entered.

'Congratulate me, Clive,' he crowed. 'When I retire from the army, I have a future in civvy street as a sleuth.'

Clive raised an ironic eyebrow. 'You do surprise me, Albert. Am I to gather you have some news for me?'

Albert sat. 'Indeed, Clive. The man you seek is named Toplis, Percy Toplis. His last known sighting on Army property was on Boxing Day. He was seen driving out of the Army Service Corps depot at Bulford in a Sunbeam motor car - property of the War Office and valued at one hundred pounds.'

'How on earth,' Clive began. Albert held up an admonitory

finger. 'He was dressed in a captain's uniform so went unchallenged at the gate. The car, needless to say, has vanished. Two days later, Toplis was spotted in Bath dressed in sergeant-major's uniform and carousing with a young woman. A sharp-eyed military policeman spotted them boarding the Bristol train at Bath railway station. While he was unable to get to the rogue's carriage before the train pulled out, he used the railway company's telegraph system to send a wire to Bristol, alerting the military authorities there. When the train arrived, Toplis was arrested.'

'And?' Clive asked.

Albert frowned. 'As the local garrison detention cells were packed, he was put under lock and key in an overspill guardroom. On his second night there, he persuaded his gaolers – two witless boys – to join him in a game of pontoon. At about midnight, one of the guards left to make the log entry. On his return, he found Toplis holding his comrade's gun. Having locked them both in his cell, he vanished into the night. No sign of him since. I rather think he has made his way to London and is lying low.' Albert sighed unhappily.

'But surely now that Bow Street Magistrate's Court is dealing with deserters from all three services, isn't it just a matter of time before he is arrested by the police?'

'Unfortunately not, Clive. Few constables on the beat would dare stop a commissioned officer or senior N.C.O. for questioning. It seems that he has quite a reputation for appearing in officers' uniforms and making off with petroleum, tyres, motor oil and batteries. It's uncanny. I understand that he has never been caught red-handed and he disposes of his haul only to unscrupulous middlemen. They sell it on to commercial users such as the owners of motor lorries, taxi cab firms and so forth at an attractive price, which they explain by claiming the 'goods' are either bankrupt stock or seizures by Customs and Excise Officers.'

'How on earth are such large quantities of liquid stolen?' Clive asked querulously. 'After all, the bally stuff comes in gallon tin cans, doesn't it?'

'It does, yes. But what happens is that a corrupt driver of a military transport vehicle arrives at an Army depot to deliver empty petrol tins and collect full ones, for which the driver signs a receipt. On his way back he makes a detour to some den of thieves. There a number of full tins are removed from the centre of the load and empty tins take their place. When they arrive at the home barracks they are unloaded by complicit soldiers.'

'And what have the quartermaster sergeants have to say about all this?' Clive demanded.

'They have absolutely nothing to say, Clive, as to them it is an Army Services Corps problem. Though the avoidance of waste is within their bailiwick, they are all from an earlier age of transport. They know how many feeds can be had from a sack of oats or a bale of hay, and what the daily water requirements of horses and mules are. As regards the rate of petroleum consumption, they are as ignorant as am I. So, there we are, Clive. I am sorry I can't be more helpful.'

'On the contrary, Albert, you have been most informative,' Clive replied grimly. 'And thank you in particular for pointing out the deficiencies of the quartermasters. I shall be meeting Sir Henry in an hour and he will be pleased to have a stick with which to beat the Quartermaster General when the time is right.'

He brooded. 'From what you have gleaned so far, Albert, perhaps you might put together a Toplis biography, so to speak. It could be most helpful when it comes to bringing that thief to justice.'

'Certainly, Clive. It might take a little time though. There are quite a number of separate records and sources to check.'

'Such as?'

Albert smiled. 'The Army, the Admiralty and the Royal Flying Corps, Clive. Many, many records.'

ooooo0OOOOooooo

On leaving McKeever's office in Fownes Street, Waite walked the short distance through Dublin's commercial centre to Burgh Quay. Reflecting on the successful outcome of this, his first ever business appointment, he realised he could build on it to secure new clients. He was close to the river Liffey. There was a wide bridge some yards to his right leading northwards to a handsome thoroughfare. Gazing at the dark green waters below, he guessed that the river was about a third the width of the Thames. A couple of hundred yards upriver to his left, an elegant arched metal footbridge was busy with pedestrians crossing both ways. A barge, black smoke pouring from a man-sized funnel, was steaming downriver. He watched its progress to the main bridge.

Jack had intended staying on the tram until it reached the terminus at Nelson's Pillar in Sackville Street but on a whim he got off at D'Olier Street. Turning left at the Ballast Office corner, he walked a little distance along Burgh Quay and crossed to the quayside. A little further on, some jarveys stood smoking and chatting alongside their sidecars. At the quay wall, a fella with time on his hands was gawking up the river. It struck Jack that his face looked familiar. Who was he? Definitely nobody he had met so far in Dublin. Curious, he dodged through the traffic, careful to avoid the horse shit on the roadway. The man was now looking down at a passing barge. Closer, Jack's eyes widened. It was the officer who had been his Soldier's Friend at that court martial. He smiled involuntarily. Following sentencing, Jack had been marched straight back down to the cellars and had never had a chance to thank the officer for getting him off the desertion charge. He could do it now, he resolved. Why not? Who knew either of them had last met at a court martial? Apart from the Volunteer officers he dealt with and his own boss Skipper Wright and other bookies, no one knew anything about Jack Kelly. His 'Officer Friend' had been a second lieutenant then. But what the deuce was his name?

As the barge steamed closer, Waite saw it was stacked end to end with barrels. Thick black smoke poured from a thin funnel jutting up at the stern and soon dissipated in the light wind. A bargee stood on the narrow passageway between the top of the wheelhouse and the narrow edge of the deck. At the stern another man stood, his hand on the tiller, as the craft steamed smartly for the centre stone arch of the main bridge. Waite's initial idle curiosity as to whether or not the funnel would hit the highest centre arch became fascination. Just before the barge nosed under the arch two of the bargees ducked low over the barrels. The third, standing upright beside the funnel, looked intently ahead. Just as it seemed the funnel was certain to hit the arch, the bargee pulled it back to lie flat on the wheelhouse roof. It was hinged. Clever! Waite smiled. In seconds, billowing clouds of black smoke poured out in its wake as it passed under the bridge.

'Hello, Lieutenant, Sir.'

Waite froze. Someone here in Dublin had recognised him. Dammit! Was the game up before it had hardly begun? He turned. A smiling young man stood beside him. His face was vaguely familiar.

'Sorry, Sir. Did I surprise you?'

Waite forced a smile. 'Not at all, my mind was on the barge. I expected its funnel to hit the bridge.'

'That makes a pair of us, Sir!'

Waite, thinking rapidly, could neither recall the young man's name nor where and when they had last met. 'I'm no longer a lieutenant, I ended service on demobilization as captain.' He looked curiously at Jack. 'And your name is?'

'Jack Kelly, Sir.'

'Where did we meet?'

'Five years ago now, Sir. At that court martial. In France. You got me off.' Jack beamed.

'Yes, of course. How could I have forgotten? My first and only court martial!'

'It was my first one too, Sir.'

They laughed. Jack was pleased his latest name had been accepted without question.

Waite thrust out his hand. 'I'm delighted to see you again, Jack.'

'And I'm very glad to meet you too, Sir. I never had a chance to thank you for saving me from the firing squad.'

'It was my pleasure ... no-one was more surprised than myself, I can tell you, but let's not look that gift horse in the mouth. We were lucky to have a kind and honourable man conducting the court martial.' Waite was expansive in relief. 'Why don't we go somewhere for a cup of tea? Or perhaps you'd prefer a drink?'

'I don't drink, Captain.'

'I'm ordinary Mr. Lexington again now, Jack. Now about that cup of tea... well, you see I don't know Dublin. It's my first day here on a quick visit – I'm here on insurance business – and then I go back to London on tonight's sailing from Kingstown. Where do you recommend we go?'

Relieved to hear that Lexington was unknown to anyone in Dublin, Jack quickly picked a place with no chance of any Shinners he knew being there.

'I'd say the Four Courts' Hotel. It's a respectable place and it's only a little walk up the quays.'

'Good. Let's head for there, then,' Waite said.

ooooo0OOO0ooooo

Chapter 3

'...the enemies of order (in Ireland) are dangerous not merely
(because) of their fanaticism, numbers and audacity but
because of their brains. An enemy that enjoys apparently large
resources of money, an admirable intelligence department ... is
truly a formidable force in the land. If he is not stopped with
strength, the versatility and imagination at least equal to his
own, his successes will be frequent and disconcerting.'

The Irish Times, 5th April 1920

Waite sat on the overstuffed sofa in Cromie's office. It was his first 'debrief' session. Cromie's spectacles reflected the light from the window, making it impossible for Waite to see his expression.

'Now then, tell me, Waite, how exactly does Jack get his information?'

'From certain ex-servicemen, men he says he can trust.'

'Have you met any of them?'

'No. I did suggest it once but he said it wasn't a good idea.'

'Why?'

'He said his informants would run a mile if they thought whoever was getting their information wanted to see them.'

'Well, I suppose that's understandable enough, given their type.' Cromie removed a cigarette from the box on the low table between them and offered one to Waite. He continued, 'There's one thing in particular that I'd like to know from Jack and it's this. Apart from the names and addresses he sends to London, has he given you any reason to believe he knows the yields we get from the raids we carry out?'

'I don't think so - it never occurred to me to ask him.' Waite paused. 'If I did ask him, don't you think he would ask for more cash?'

'Yes, I suppose he might. Speaking of money, how much does he give these men?'

'To each man?'

'Yes.'

'It varies. He tells me it could be anything from five shillings to fifteen shillings.'

'Why the different amounts?'

'He said it depends on the ex-servicemen. He says they are not saints. He said he has a few tricky ones but he's unwilling to drop them in case they go to the other side and sell him out – his words.'

'Well, that might explain the varying quality of the information we've gotten so far.'

Cromie lapsed into silence.

'Are you not satisfied with the information that Jack is getting?' Waite asked.

'On the contrary, Waite, he's one of our better sources inside the Sinn Féin camp. So we need to ... to cultivate him. Or rather cultivate his contacts.'

Alert, Waite noted the phrase '... one of our better sources.' So he, Waite, was after all just one of a number of Stepney novices based here in Dublin. 'Cultivate? I don't understand, Sir.'

'Some of his offerings are, so to speak, the scrapings of the barrel but you've explained that. However, one or two of his informants seem to be delivering really good stuff.'

'Good stuff?'

'In addition to bagging seventeen more Volunteers, a few more Mausers, two Mills bombs and a Stokes round, the latest trawl of his addresses yielded a parcel with 100 copies of *An Thuglock* addressed to one of their Volunteer Commandants – as they style their local bandit officers – in Limerick.'

'That's rather a good haul, isn't it, Sir?'

'Oh indeed, yes.' Cromie leaned forward. 'I want you to persuade Jack – without jeopardising himself or his sources – to pay particular attention to any information on the two top terrorists we must get our hands on – Mulcahy and Collins – dead or alive. Remind him that his informants are assured of a handsome reward, safe passage and a new life somewhere congenial in the dominions or colonies if these key terrorists are captured ... or otherwise rendered ineffective to our satisfaction. And, needless to say, Jack too will be well rewarded.'

'What about that fellow with the Spanish name, em, Davilera?' Waite asked. 'I have read about him in the newspapers. I understand he is the only rebel leader to have escaped the firing squad after the 1916 Rebellion in Dublin?'

'Ah, yes, De Valera. Edward – or Eamon de Valera as he calls himself. In 1916, Maxwell, for once, had the wit to stay his hand and not shoot an American citizen. You see, although de Valera's mother was Irish and his father either a Spaniard or a Cuban, he was born in New York and so he is a U.S. citizen. Indeed, he is there now collecting more money for the Shinners. That said, we're not too bothered about him. He is a moderate Sinn Féiner.'

'A moderate Sinn Féiner! Is there such a thing?'

'There are more of them than you'd think.' Cromie rose and crossed to the window. 'Earlier this year, in an interview for the *Westminster Gazette,* de Valera stated that Ireland and Great Britain can come to a peaceful arrangement whereby our strategic naval interests in Ireland are protected in the same way as those between the United States and Cuba. Yet, for all that, his begging bowl efforts to collect funds for Sinn Féin continue in America. According to our best estimates he has so far collected well over $3 million which is earning interest in some New York bank account way beyond our reach in law.'

'Are you saying there are Shinners in the United States?' Waite enquired.

'Oh, yes, but over there they go by the name of *Clan na Gael.'* He paused. 'There are ten times more Irish-Americans in the whole of the United States than there are Irish living in Ireland. We must concern ourselves with the job of getting on top of the Shinners here. Forget de Valera for now, Collins and Mulcahy are our top targets. I don't know if you are aware that there's a reward of £10,000 for Collins dead or alive.'

'I haven't seen any posters stating that, Sir?'

'And you won't. This is the United Kingdom, not Buffalo Bill's Wild West. We can't put the name of an elected Member of Parliament on a 'Wanted' poster!'

Waite was aghast. 'Collins is a Member of Parliament?'

'Oh, yes. He and Mulcahy and almost all the rest of their rebel Dáil assembly are also elected Members of Parliament. Mind you, not all are gunmen as, thankfully, there are quite a few moderates like de Valera. But the gunmen now have the upper hand with, it seems, Collins and Mulcahy ruling the roost. If we can catch one or the other or, ideally, both of them, get our hands on the Shinners' cash here and also on the printing presses churning out the Thuglock and the *Irish Bulletin*, then the Shinners' whole rotten house of cards will collapse, allowing the moderates to take over.'

'That seems a tall order, Sir,' Waite ventured.

'Listen, Waite, *ad astra semper.* Always aim high. You may not get all you seek but you may end up with more than you expected.'

'I'll do my damnedest, Sir, I assure you,' Waite said.

'Good man! You're going across to Dublin on the mailboat tonight, aren't you?'

'Yes, Sir, I am.'

'Well, your focus is to send Jack single-mindedly after Mulcahy and Collins.

ooooo0000ooooo

Bewley's Tea Rooms, Westmoreland Street, Dublin.

So Percy Toplis was dead! Jack held the newspaper closer. Poor old Percy. His luck had run out at last. He had chanced his arm once too often. But shot dead? He re-read and repeated the report to himself: '... in an exchange of gunfire with armed police.' Yes, definitely the police and not Army redcaps. The redcaps never carried guns unless on guard duties or during a mutiny like the one in Étaples. Putting the newspaper back on the chair where he had found it, he realized that he would never have known Percy had copped it if he hadn't picked it up. He glanced around the tea rooms. Bewley's wasn't the place where you'd expect to find a working man, not surprising given the price of a pot of tea. He was impressed that this was the place he had been told to meet the captain. Someone was using his head, he couldn't imagine a snooping Peeler coming in here. Any well-dressed fellow was a respectable gent to a Peeler. Not once had Jack been stopped in the street by a Peeler since Percy told him what clothes to wear and when and how to speak proper. He took another sip of tea. Yes, Percy was great at the posh accents and the manners of toffs. When Percy wore civvy dress it was always gentleman's day clothes – pinched of course. That was when he was 'on other business' as he called cashing dud cheques or pawning stolen property! Nobody, he reflected, here in Bewley's or anywhere else in Dublin for that matter, would have given Percy Toplis a second glance.

Jack was mildly surprised to realise that he wasn't actually that upset to hear about Percy. Something had happened to him when Pat, his army mate, had been shot dead in no-man's-land. Since then, Jack cared for no-one except himself. His father and mother – whoever they were - hadn't cared about him. At six years of age, the nuns had sent him from the orphanage to Trim Reformatory. Nine years there and then he had been sent to that bachelor uncle. And a right mean old bastard and slave driver he was too. Was he even a real uncle at all? He never mentioned Jack's mother once, not even to slag her. Then the Army were glad to have him even though he was underage. But everything changed when it turned on him – the very Army he'd volunteered to join. He wasn't let go to Pat's burial. Instead, they wanted to shoot him as a deserter for trying to help his friend. Yeah, he really was lucky at his court martial to have a Prisoner's Friend like Mr. Lexington – definitely not his real name, Jack reflected. A decent sort for an English officer but, back then, he was wet behind the ears and knew nothing about military law. But he listened carefully to Jack repeating what the few old sweats had told him to say. They knew back-to-front every Army Regulation that really mattered to serving men and especially the court martial rules. He would have ended six foot under just like his mate Pat but for Mr. Lexington speaking up for him. And it helped too that the sergeant who reported him was in hospital with a gunshot wound. So instead of a firing squad, he was sentenced to three months detention for being absent without leave. When that was up, he was despatched to the detention huts in Étaples to join the rest of the 'boys' in the Bantam Battalion compound there. And then there was the mutiny.

'Ah! There you are, Jack!' Captain Price slipped into the booth beside him. 'We have a job for you. You're not from Dublin and you're not known around, apart from your bookie work.' Price smiled as a waitress placed a cup on the table in front of him. 'We get all sorts in the Volunteers,' he went on. 'And there's one or two we're a bit uneasy about.'

'How many Volunteers are there?' Jack asked.

'Over 100,000 at the last count, that is across the whole country.'

'100,000! That's more than double the British Army here now, isn't it?'

'In numbers, yeah.' He looked enquiringly at Jack. 'Has anybody filled you in on the Volunteers? Do you know how

71

it's organised?'

'Nobody in the Birr Volunteers told me anything about that.' He paused. 'And I didn't ask.'

'Wise man! The Irish Volunteers – *Oglaigh na hÉireann* – has exactly the same basic structure as any army today: Command, Division, Brigade, Battalion and finally Company with active service units.'

'Ogleenaherren?' Jack was intrigued.

'It's the Irish for Warriors or Soldiers of Ireland.'

'But the English newspapers call them the Sinn Féin Volunteers?'

'They're wrong,' Price said. 'Sinn Féin is a separate political organisation. The British Press can't be bothered with the difference. Anyone opposing the Crown is a Sinn Féiner to them.'

'So I am an ogleenaherren Volunteer?' Jack tried on the unfamiliar word for size.

'Yes, you are. You're in the Finglas Volunteer Company.'

'Finglas - that's out in the country, isn't it?'

'It is. Most Volunteers don't know any Volunteers from outside their unit area. The only person in Finglas who knows of your existence is the Company O.C.'

'Why?' Jack said cautiously.

'Firstly, because you've been on ... confidential duties. And secondly, you're a deserter from the British Army.'

Jack was irate. 'But that's the enemy, isn't it? Wasn't it a good thing to do?'

'Yes, of course. Like everywhere else, there are always a few Volunteers with big heads and little minds. They think any Irishman who joined the British army was a traitor in the first place.'

'But I was conscripted in England. I couldn't do anything about it.' Jack found the lies coming naturally. 'And even if I had gone back to Ireland to avoid it, they would have been looking out for me as a deserter.'

'I know, I know, Jack. Indeed I well remember how different it was in 1914 when droves of young fellas all over the country joined up to fight for the freedom of little Catholic Belgium.'

'And I stuck my neck out to help the Volunteers when I was in Crinkle Barracks.' Jack was now feeling quite hard done by.

'You did indeed, Jack. But the enemy has its own intelligence officers trying to find out all they can about us. And we had to be sure you weren't sent by them.'

'You mean you didn't trust me?'

'You'd be a fool to completely trust someone offering information and not asking for payment.' The captain regarded him coolly.

'I didn't go to them for money,' Jack protested. 'I was picked out in Birr by an officer and asked to help out. And I did. So if the Army caught me at it then – or now - I'd be in the Glass House for ten years at least.'

'I know that, Jack. Your Volunteer superior officers know that.

But that is all confidential information and is no business of rank and file Volunteers in Birr, Finglas or anywhere else.' He paused. 'You see, some of them seem to think they're running this war. And, like I said, they regard Irishmen like you who are British army ex-serviceman, with suspicion.'

'Are you saying that the Volunteers can decide who joins up and who doesn't?'

'Yes.' He paused. 'It is a real Volunteer army, Jack. The Volunteers elect their own officers. And, of course, Command can't order any Volunteer into battle.'

Mouth open in disbelief, Jack looked at the captain and then slowly repeated his words.

'They elect their own officers and can't be ordered into battle?'

'Yes.'

Astonished, Jack was speechless. Then for some reason Percy came to mind. And knowing what he'd say, Jack couldn't help blurting out. 'I shoulda joined the Volunteers before I got conscripted.'

'What did you just say!'

'I said I shoulda joined the Volunteers before I was conscripted, Sir!'

After a few seconds of charged silence, they burst out laughing. Sobering, the Captain glanced around. 'There are other things you should know. Volunteers are not entitled to any pay. They must buy their own uniforms. They are also required to make a contribution of sixpence a week to help pay for the overall cost of the organisation.'

74

'I didn't know they have uniforms, Sir.'

'Those that can afford them, yes. And Volunteers are also expected to contribute to the cost of their personal weapons.'

Jack's frown conveyed respectful attention while masking an emerging nagging doubt. How could this lot win against a paid, trained, full-time and better equipped regular army? Did he want to be around if and when it all went wrong?

'Anyway, what the Volunteers around the country are doing doesn't concern you,' Captain Price continued. 'But – and this is important – because of the confidential duties you are about to undertake, you will be required to take an oath of secrecy and make a solemn commitment to the Irish Republic. Do you have religious scruples?'

Jack looked doubtful. "Don't think so, sir,' he said cautiously.

'Right. Now you have to take the oath.' The Captain took a small piece of folded paper from his pocketbook and opened it out. 'Repeat this after me as quietly as you can.'

'In the presence of God, I, Jack Kelly, do solemnly swear that I will do my utmost to establish the Independence of Ireland, and that I will bear true allegiance to the Supreme Council of the Irish Republican Brotherhood and the Government of the Irish Republic and implicitly obey the constitution of the Irish Republican Brotherhood and all my superior officers and that I will preserve the secrets of the organisation.'

When they had finished, the captain grasped Jack's hand. Jack felt the press of a finger knuckle against his palm. 'Welcome, Brother Jack, to the Organisation. That's the handshake you use to check if a fellow is one of us.' Releasing his grip, he continued. 'That is one of the first recognition signs – Brother to Brother only – of the Organisation. Remember it. You will be instructed in further recognition signs when I introduce you to your first Circle parade.'

'Circle parade?'

'All in due course, Jack.'

'I'm a Volunteer now?'

'You are, Jack.' The captain smiled.

'Right so. I suppose now is the time to tell you about the British ex-army officer I bumped into who asked me to get any information I could about the Volunteers.'

'What!'

ooooo0000oooooo

Kate left the offices of Michael Noyk, Solicitor, in College Green, a Dáil Éireann cheque for £36 in her purse bearing his signature, as a trustee of Dáil funds. Intended as payment for the first six months rent of a second floor office premises on the north Dublin quays, Mr Noyk would arrange for a modest brass nameplate bearing the name of a small accountancy practice to be affixed to the front door. It was one of three duplicate offices of the Dáil Minister for Labour, Countess Markievicz. In common with the other outlawed ministries, this one would have files and records identical to those in both other offices in case of raids by the Dublin Castle authorities.

Kate had been fascinated by Constance Markievicz from the first time she had seen the tall, striking woman striding around Dublin. She had rebelled against the stifling Victorian conventions of her Anglo-Irish landowning family to support in turn the Suffragettes, Socialism and the Citizen Army of James Connolly. She had learned to drill and fire a gun alongside Dubliners who had fought in the Boer War with the British Army. When the Irish Volunteers were formed in 1913, women were not permitted to join. Constance, nothing daunted, became Deputy Commandant of the Citizen Army force in the 1916 Rebellion, was convicted by court martial and imprisoned in England. On her release, she was elected a Westminster M.P. on the Sinn Féin ticket – the first ever women elected to Parliament in British history.

Kate believed that Countess Markievicz, as President of Cumann na mBan, the women's auxiliary of the Volunteers, disapproved of the Cumann's inevitable subordination to the Volunteers. That said, Kate, although herself a member of Sinn Féin, had never had the slightest interest in joining the women's Cumann. Her years in a convent boarding-school had provided her with sufficient military discipline for life. And certain of the Cumann ladies were a little, well, intense in their dedication to the cause.

She was already at O'Connell Bridge. She would make a quick visit to Noblet's for Mama's secret treat – a small bag of sugar-dusted bon-bons. Then she would visit the gleaming new premises of Eason's stationer, bookseller and lending library, transformed from the smoking ruin it had been after the Rebellion four years earlier.

ooooo0000oooooo

77

'One, two, three, four, one, two, three, four, one, two, three, four, that's it, Signor Lexington, you have got it correct nearly. So let us continue to the finish.' Waite, perspiring, conducted the portly Signor Basagni in his role as 'lady' around the latter's Dancing Academy in Mountjoy Square. He despaired of mastering the intricacies of ballroom dancing. Perhaps if he had started to learn when younger, he thought, he might have had more aptitude. Dancing lessons had been close to non-existent in his minor public school. He was barely two weeks home in Simla on completing his education when the War began. Throughout his six years of military service, the only 'social events' for officers were those rare occasions in an improvised mess for drinks, army gossip and, perhaps, a game of cards. In common with many young officers holding temporary commissions, Waite was barely able to pay his mess fees, servants' gratuities and so on. Leave periods passed frugally with no opportunities for dancing.

Once settled in Dublin, and always hopeful of meeting Miss Swanton again – Dublin was such a small place, everybody said so, it surely must happen sooner or later – he had vowed not to embarrass himself in front of her if the ability to dance were to be required. He did feel, however, that this, his fourth lesson, was proving to be just a little less of a nightmare than the previous three. Practising in his lodgings, where the carpet was thankfully thick, had led to greater competence, at least while dancing with an imaginary partner, when he found himself with considerable grace and fluidity of movement. Lessons with Signor Basagni, however, highlighted his tendency to centrifugal and possibly centripetal pirouettes. For all his theatricality, the Italian was a perfectionist. Waite sighed. A few more lessons, and hopefully he would be confident enough to acquit himself on the dance floor.

Twenty arduous minutes later Signor Basagni declared himself satisfied with his pupil's progress, lifted the gramophone needle, and Waite escaped.

His spirits rose as he headed towards Sackville Street. At the intersection with Abbey Street, he checked the time on Eason's wall-clock opposite. He had two business calls to make, and then it would be time for a spot of lunch. By this time, he had become accustomed to his new role as insurance agent. His discovery of Thom's Directory, which listed businesses street by street, had helped with the tedium of canvassing. His by now impressive record of businesses visited ought to satisfy any Shinner busybody who might decide to inspect his small office in his absence.

As his glance dropped to the shop's main entrance, his heart leaped – Miss Swanton was standing there. He crossed the street, just as she turned left. He quickened his pace. At the Henry Street corner of the ruined G.P.O. he drew alongside her.

'Miss Swanton, isn't it?'

She stopped and turned. 'Well, if it isn't ... Mr Lexington!' she smiled.

'I do apologise for accosting you in the street like this, but then it is not as if we were absolute strangers,' Waite stammered.

'But we are absolute strangers, Mr Lexington, by...'

As she paused, his heart dropped. Damn. He had been too forward. Too familiar.

'...by the standards of our parents' generation. Wouldn't you

79

agree?'

'Oh, yes, certainly,' he beamed.

Waite became aware that he was grinning like an idiot. He should act quickly before she moved away. 'Might I suggest that we go for morning coffee? That is, if you have the time?'

She glanced at her fob watch. 'I do have about a half an hour to spare – that would be rather nice.'

Waite looked around wildly. 'Might I suggest that we go to the Gresham Hotel – it's quite near?'

'We could indeed go there, it is an excellent hotel – but it would be quite crowded with businessmen at this time, don't you think?' There, she had lied once more. The Gresham wouldn't be so crowded now, but it was a preferred social venue among senior Sinn Féin men and Cumann na mBan women. Although an English accent such as Mr Lexington's was not at all out of the ordinary in Dublin, she had no wish for a nosey Nationalist to join them, or to eavesdrop.

'Well, there are other hotels on this side of the street,' Waite responded happily. 'Which would you recommend?'

'I rather think the Hamman Hotel might be suitable,' Kate said. 'It's rather old-fashioned, but it is quiet.' And it was avoided by 'advanced Nationalists' because of its largely Irish Unionist clientele.

They settled into comfortable seats in the hotel lounge over a pot of tea. 'Have you settled into your business now, Mr Lexington?' Kate enquired.

'Yes, indeed, thank you.' Waite found himself tongue-tied.

The idea of insurance as a topic of conversation had never occurred to him.

'I imagine insurance is a competitive business?' Kate strove to get the conversational ball rolling.

Waite seized on this. 'Oh, it certainly is,' he said. 'And with costs rising every other day, businessmen are not automatically renewing their cover with the same firm.'

'So you're not engaged in providing personal insurance? You know, life assurance, home insurance?'

'Thankfully not, Miss Swanton.'

'Why thankfully?'

Waite swallowed. 'Because I am rarely required to call on commercial clients in the evenings or after midday on Saturday. That gives me evenings and most of the weekend free for – other things.'

Kate looked thoughtful. 'I hadn't thought of evening and weekend work,' she said. 'I shouldn't like to have to work such hours either.' Another fib to add to the mounting list, considering her Dáil Éireann work. 'And do firms write to you or to your company in London requesting estimates?' she enquired.

'That can happen, but not very often, I'm told,' Waite said earnestly. 'Most of the time, such enquiries come from men who will stay with their current insurer but will flourish the estimate of a competitor to beat down the premium they have been quoted. My chances of renewal business are far less if they contact me first.'

'That certainly seems to be challenging commercial work, Mr Lexington. Unlike mine, as an apprentice solicitor. And messenger girl.' Seeing his uncomprehending expression, she went on hurriedly. 'As an apprentice in my uncle's practice I have to draw up outline drafts of bills, contracts and so forth. I must also draft summaries of cases for clients and, of course, key points for counsel. Believe me, it can become quite boring. Yet I do get out of the office when certain documents cannot be entrusted to the post.'

'They must be terribly important. Or valuable?' Waite ventured.

'Well yes, they might be head leases or conveyances or, occasionally an original Last Will and Testament. One would be reluctant to entrust them to the Post Office.' She sighed. 'So that is why I am occasionally obliged to travel to London or Liverpool to deliver or collect such documents.' Concealing embarrassment at her biggest whopper so far, she looked down at her watch. 'Gracious! It's almost midday. I really must go now, Mr Lexington.'

Waite took a deep breath. 'Might we possibly meet for lunch, Miss Swanton? Perhaps tomorrow?'

'That would be lovely,' Kate smiled.

'Say, one o'clock at the Hibernian Hotel in Dawson Street?

'That would be perfect,' she rose to go.

'I look forward to it,' Waite beamed.

ooooo0OOOOooooo

The dimly lit back room of the Talbot Street tailor's shop smelled of the cloth lying in rolls on deep shelves. Three tailor's dummies took up most of the floor space, each with the makings of men's jackets cut and pinned in place. Jack went to open the window. He regarded the backs of the Abbey Street buildings directly opposite. A shared lane separated what he guessed must have once been long narrow gardens on both sides. That lane would be a handy way out if the police raided the tailor's shop, he mused. He chuckled as he recalled the shock on the captain's face when he had dropped the Lexington bombshell. He started and stared at Jack. Then, visibly controlling himself, he spoke casually. 'Well, that's very interesting. However, that's something you'll have to tell my senior officer in person.'

'Alright, Sir,' Jack said agreeably.

'Right,' Price rose. 'Let's go.'

Once on the street, the captain led the way at a fast clip. Jack struggled to keep up, dodging pedestrians. They turned right at Nelson's Pillar and continued on towards Talbot Street. The captain stopped outside a shop with *The Republican Tailors* over the door. Inside, the captain spoke in Irish to the man behind the counter. He turned to Jack. 'A senior officer will be coming to have a chat with you shortly, O.K.?'

'Of course, yes, Sir.'

'Best that you wait upstairs. I'm off now.' Pausing, the captain chuckled. 'You'll be in good hands.'

Jack followed the other fellow up three flights of stairs until they reached the top landing. Opening the single door there, the tailor motioned him to enter. Barely a pace or two inside, he heard the door behind him slam shut. The key turned in the lock. They still didn't trust him. Shrugging, he sat down on one of the chairs there and waited.

Some time later he heard footsteps on the stairs. Glancing at his watch, he figured he had been waiting for nearly three-quarters of an hour. A tap on the door was followed by the sound of the key turning. A muscular-looking man in his late twenties entered. Closing the door he turned and, smiling, held out his hand.

'I'm Frank Staunton. Pleased to meet you, Jack.'

As they shook hands, Jack was surprised to feel the knuckle in his palm – exactly the same as the captain's grip. What was he to say?

'Hello, Brother,' Jack said cautiously.

'Let's get down to business and have a chat.' He took a seat facing Jack. 'They tell me you've been a very satisfactory Volunteer.'

'I'm doing me best, Sir.'

'Before we talk about ... other matters, I'd like to hear all about you from yourself. So, let's begin from when you were born.'

'I think I was born somewhere in Roscommon in 1900. But I'm not sure. I don't have a birth certificate and I don't know anything about my father or my mother.'

'You were an orphan then, God help you?'

'Yeah,' Jack paused. 'I was taken as a baby to an orphanage run by nuns and kept there until I was six or seven.'

He always stopped at this point and looked down at the floor for a while. Nobody ever seemed to want any more details of that time and this fellow was no different.

'So what about schooling, Jack?'

'The nuns there had a junior infants' school for local children beside the orphanage and I went there until I was about seven, I think. Then they sent me to the boys' reformatory in Trim and I was there until I finished classes when I was nearly fifteen.'

'Where did you go then?'

'They told me at Trim that there was a job for me on my uncle's farm in Roscommon. As it was only 30 acres or so they said my uncle told them he didn't need a labourer but just a helping hand. He was...'

'Just a minute, Jack. Where was this farm?'

'Near the town of Boyle – that's in County Roscommon.'

'What was the name of the town land?'

'Sroankeeragh, I think or something like that.'

'Was that the town land or the parish name?'

'I don't know.'

'What's your Uncle's name?'

'Bill Mernagh.'

'O.K. Go on.'

'Well, he turned out to be a nasty old miser. He had me working day and night in the farmyard and in his fields for seven days a week. And for all of that he paid me sixpence a day because he said I was getting free food and lodgings. I put up with his slavery for nearly three years and in the meantime I saved up the sixpences. Then one day, he gave me a bad clout over the ear for nothing and I decided that I had enough of him. So a few days later I took meself off.'

'You left?'

'Yes, Sir, I did. I walked eleven miles to the nearest railway station for to get a train to Dublin. When I got there I was on the next boat outa there for Liverpool.'

'Why Liverpool?'

'I knew there'd be no RIC men looking out for me there.'

'And why would the RIC be interested in you?'

Jack looked mutinous. 'Because before I left, I took a few sovereigns from his hidey-hole. He owed me wages for three years.' He glanced under his brows at Staunton. He seemed unimpressed.

'Did you know anybody in Liverpool?'

'No.'

'What did you do when you got there?'

'I made for the nearest Catholic church and talked to one of the priests. He fixed me up with an Irish couple whose two sons were in France. They helped me to get a live-in job as a house boy in a big house in the country. And then eight months later I was conscripted.'

'How old were you then?'

'I had just turned eighteen.'

Staunton looked away. Jack felt ill at ease. Would he want the name and address of the big house? He'd best think of a name fast.

'O.K, Jack, that's enough of that for now. So now tell me about this Lexington fellow.'

Jack relaxed. The rest would be easy.

'Were you in his regiment during the war?'

'No, I wasn't in his regiment, Sir. I don't know what his regiment was. When I came across him he was lying in the mud. That was after we attacked the German lines but that didn't come off. Men from different regiments had got mixed up when they were trying to find their way back to their own lines, with mortar shells exploding and machine gun bullets everywhere. I came across him wounded and with his leg caught in a loop of barbed wire. I got him untangled but he said we'd better stay there until after dark. So as soon as it was dark I helped him along to a forward casualty station. It took ages. As soon as they took him in, an officer told me I wasn't needed anymore and ordered me to return to my regiment. I never saw him again until I bumped into him here in Dublin.'

'And he remembered your face after all that time?'

'Well, Sir, why wouldn't he? When we were laying low, it must have been for five or six hours, he could see my face all the time.'

87

'Alright,' Staunton said. 'Go on.'

'Well, when I met him here, Mr. Lexington insisted on taking me for dinner. He called it lunch.'

'Where?'

'In the Four Courts Hotel. After that he asked me was I interested in helping ex-servicemen around here who were being badly treated by the Sinn Féiners.'

'What exactly did he say?'

'Well, you know, something like 'speaking as one old soldier to another' was the way he put it.'

'And what did you say?'

'I said, "Certainly, Sir." That's what he wanted to hear, wasn't it?'

Staunton gazed at him keenly. 'What did he want from you?'

'He wanted any information on the Volunteers I could get.'

'Such as?'

'The names and addresses of any Volunteers. And any information about where Volunteer guns and ammunition were stored.' He paused. 'And there were certain Volunteers they want badly.'

'Did he say any names?'

'He mentioned ... let me think ... yes ... Mulcaire. And Collins.'

'Mulcaire? That wouldn't have been Mulcahy, would it?'

'Come to think about it, yeah, it was Mulcahy, Sir.'

'Do you know who they are?'

'No. I never heard of them before.'

'Did he offer you money?'

Jack hesitated, then gazed at Staunton with guileless eyes. 'He did but I said no.'

'Why?'

'I'd be on their army pay list again, wouldn't I, Sir?'

'Why would that bother you?'

'Because I'm a British Army deserter, Sir! I told Captain Price that.'

'Yes, of course. But you didn't tell him – Lexington I mean – that you were a deserter?'

Jack looked at Staunton in disbelief. 'I'm not simple, Sir.'

He paused. 'You told Captain Price that Lexington only contacts you when he is in Dublin?'

'That's right, Mr. Staunton.'

'Who does he work for?'

'The British Army, I suppose.'

'No, what's his front?'

'Front?'

'His cover job?'

'He never mentioned anything about what he was doing in Dublin.' Jack paused. 'Oh, yeah, he did say he was just visiting Dublin for the day. I think he said something to do with business insurance here.'

'Right. What do you have to do if you want to get in touch with him urgently?'

'I'm to post a letter to him at the India Club in London.'

'Where is that?'

Taking a small notebook from his pocket, Jack read it out. 'Mr S. Lexington, India Club, Aldwych, London E.C.'

Staunton scribbled on a piece of paper. 'Now tell me how he is to get in touch with you if and when he wants to meet you. Or if you need to meet him?'

'He'll send me a letter telling me to meet him at the Gresham Hotel on a certain day and time and that means the day before at the Royal Hibernian Hotel at the same time.'

Staunton remained silent for a minute or so.

'You told Captain Price that all Lexington wanted of you was to send any information whatsoever to a Bermondsey address. You still have that address?'

'Yeah, do you want it?'

'Yes.'

Jack read it out.

'Did he say anything else?'

'He wanted to know where he could contact me. I said I was just about to change my lodgings and he said I should write to him at the India Club when I was settled.'

'And ...?' Staunton asked.

'I didn't know what to do as I thought nobody would believe me. That is until I told the captain this morning. So will I write to him now?'

'No. Not for a few days yet. We have to handle this carefully.'

Staunton paused again, concentrating. To Jack it seemed a long time before he spoke again.

'What you'll do next is to write to him for a meeting.'

'Where?'

'Anywhere in Dublin he chooses. And when you meet him, you ask him for money.'

'Money! For what, Mr. Staunton? I told you what I told Captain Price ...'

Staunton cut across him. 'For the information you're about to start passing on to him from your ex-servicemen pals.'

'But I don't have any ex-servicemen pals.'

'Lexington doesn't know that, does he?'

'No, I suppose he doesn't.'

'So he will expect you to ask for some money, if not for

yourself, then at least for the ex-servicemen giving it.'

''Where will I get the information I'll be giving him?'

'You don't need to know that, Jack. All you will be passing on to him are names and addresses.'

'How much will I ask for?'

'Not too much, not too little. Say between one pound ten and two pounds a week to start. And of course you'll keep an account for him of what you pay out. But don't worry, we'll look after that paperwork for you so that you can show him the balance you have left at any time – in your own handwriting, of course.'

'Yes, Sir, but who will I give the money to when I get it?'

'You give it to nobody. You may need it in an emergency.'

'Right, Sir.'

'From now on don't speak to anyone about this matter. Anyone! Understand?'

'Yes, Mr. Staunton. But what will I say to Captain Price?'

'Nothing. I'll speak to him later.' He paused. 'From now on you will be reporting to me. If you meet the captain or anyone else in the Volunteers, you tell them nothing about Lexington. Understand?'

'Yes, I do, Sir. Will I still be doing the bookie's runner work?'

'Oh, yes. You'll be doing your usual job with Mr. Wright. He won't ask questions.'

Chapter 4

'..the Defence of the Realm Act is so administered (in Ireland) that, in practice, the military initiate action and control (civil administration)...'

Report to Lloyd George, 12th May 1920, by Sir Warren Fisher, Permanent Secretary to the Treasury and Head of the Civil Service.

Frank Staunton surveyed the black-clad figure with amusement. 'Well, Jack, I must say you look every inch a Christian Brother.'

They were in the sitting room of a house in the genteel suburb of Rathfarnham.

'Thanks, Mr. Staunton. You musta gone to a lot of trouble to get the suit and the priest's collar?'

'It's not a priest's collar, Jack. Their collars don't have a black line in front. You're a Brother – not our kind of Brother, the other lot. There's a lot of them around so we had no problem borrowing all you need to look like one. Everything else you'll need is in the overnight bag, O.K.?'

'O.K. Sir.'

'Right! Now sit there while I get something else for you.'

He returned holding a white plaster statue of the Virgin, about two feet high, which he placed carefully on the carpet.

'Right, you'll be delivering this to a farmhouse in a place called Saltmarsh, in Co. Wexford.

Jack eyed the statue in disbelief. 'How do I get it there, Sir?'

'A horse cab will be calling here in five minutes or so. That will take you to Westland Row railway station in time for the next train to Wexford. When you arrive at the station nearest to Saltmarsh, you'll be met by a Volunteer dressed as a priest. He'll have a motor car to take you the rest of the way.

Lifting up the statue with great care, he handed it to Jack.

94

'Now hold this like it was a baby.' Jack manoeuvred it about for the best holding position. For a hollow statue, it was heavier than he expected. Turning it carefully upside down he saw it wasn't hollow inside.

'This is solid, Mr. Staunton. No wonder it's heavy.'

Staunton smiled. 'It was hollow until it was packed to the gills with detonating powder.'

Jack stiffened his grip. He knew full well how dangerous that stuff was to handle.

'So if you drop it on a hard surface the chances are you won't hear it hit the ground. Understand?'

He wasn't an eejit that needed to be told that. 'Oh, yes, Sir,' he responded meekly.

'When you've delivered the statue there won't be time for you to catch the last train back to Dublin. So you'll be spending the night at a friendly farmhouse. The next morning someone else will take you to another town for the next train back to Dublin. Alright? On the way back, keep the clerical collar and bib on all the time until you get to Amiens Street Station. Go into a cubicle in the public lavatory there and change back to an ordinary collar - take one with you. Always have porters - or pay someone - to carry your travelling bag but never, never let go of the statue. If you have to put it down anytime, lay it down flat. When you're on the train, sit with your back to the engine with the statue flat on the seat beside you. If the compartment is full - and that's not likely at this time of a week day - then hold it on your lap in case the train brakes suddenly.'

Jack found the best way to position the statue was to have the base on the seat between his knees, with the head leaning against one or other shoulder. This way only one hand was required to keep it in position – he hoped.

'Good. And do you know what, you look the picture of holy innocence! So, will you manage?'

Jack managed a grin. 'I will, Sir. '

There was a knock on the front door. Staunton rose. 'Time to go.'

ooooo0000ooooo

It was mid-afternoon when Jack's train drew into the small railway station. He was one of the handful of passengers getting off there. Knowing he was to be met, he took his time. Taking out his overnight bag he dropped it onto the platform. Carefully removing the statue he put it resting against the bag and then slammed shut the compartment door. By now the other passengers had left the platform. He carried the statue to one of the bench seats. A few minutes later, a priest came out on to the platform and approached, smiling,

'I'm Father Celsus.' He held out his hand. Grasping it Jack felt the familiar knuckle press. Feck! He shoulda done that first! But he had the month's password ready: 'Will the men of the West fight the invader?'

'Yes, and drive him in to the sea.' There was no delay in the newcomer's answer. And the Organisation had priests in it!

'Something tells me you're a double Brother, Jack?'

A joke! Definitely not a priest.

'Yes, Father.'

'Well, Brother, I'll be taking you to ... well to where you are going. So let me have your bag while you look after the Virgin – I've a motor car outside for us.'

When they were seated in the two-seater Model 'T' Ford, Jack spoke. 'That's a very delicate statue there, eh, Father. And if there's too much jolting about, well, it could be damaged.'

Father Celsus grinned. 'Brother, I know all about the statue and its power to take me to the next world! Have no fear. I'll be watching out for every pothole so don't you worry.'

'What if we're stopped by a police patrol?

'We don't have them hereabouts. Anyway they never question the clergy. So if we are stopped just be polite and let me do the talking. O.K?'

'Yes, Father.' Jack smiled to himself. Talk about telling your granny how to suck eggs.

There wasn't a word out of Father Celsus for the next three-quarters of an hour. For Jack, this was his first real view of Irish countryside. Driving the army petroleum lorries meant your eyes were always on the winding road ahead. But now he could relax as they drove along largely deserted country lanes through rolling countryside. Most of the fields had crops of potatoes or vegetables while others were under grain. Passing through a woodland area, one side of the road ran beside a high stone wall for what seemed miles. Father Celsus broke his silence to volunteer that it was part of the huge estate of one of the local gentry. Finally, they reached the townland of Saltmarsh. Ten minutes later, they stopped outside a two-storey farmhouse in the middle of nowhere. A low rough-cut stone wall surrounded a rectangular garden overgrown by weeds. The small rusting gate was open. Jack got out and carefully lifted the statue from the back seat. Taking it to the front door, he laid it gently down on the ground. He turned on hearing the Ford drive away. For a moment, he panicked. He whirled at the rasping sound of a bolt drawn. A fellow a little older than himself opened the door.

'I have a special delivery for you.' Jack said.

'O.K. I'll look after it from now on. You can be on your way.' He picked up the statue and went back into the house. The door shut behind him.

Jack was momentarily indignant. He was trusted to carry a, yes, a bomb all the way here from Dublin and not so much as an offer of a glass of water, much less a cup of tea! Well, fuck you, Mr. Smartypants know-all, he thought, you won't want to be told how bloody dangerous that detonating powder is then, will you? Turning, he strode back along the path as the Ford completed its turn and approached him. He drew in a deep breath and then let it out in a long sigh. The War was bad enough but then they all knew the odds of a direct hit by a shell were very large. Most of the time anyway. But carrying that fucking statue was like walking around with a primed shell nose down. A soldier's lot, as Percy used to say. Jack realised he was as much a nobody in this Irish 'army' as he had been in the British one.

oooooOOOOooooo

'You'll have some more tea, Brother, won't you?'

'No thanks, Mam, I'm full now. That was a grand breakfast, thanks very much. I best be going back to the bedroom now and get me things together.' Jack smiled at the elderly woman as she all but curtseyed to him.

The farmer's wife had given him enough to feed a battalion as he sat all alone at the Victorian table covered by a real lace table cloth. He was getting first class service as a 'guest' in this farmhouse – a real farmhouse more than four times bigger than his uncle's cottage. Just goes to show what the right uniform does for you, according to Percy's view on life. Draining his teacup, he glanced at his watch. 7.50 a.m. Farm life everywhere started early, as he knew only too well. Back in the bedroom, he checked everything again. Yeah, he was ready to leave. But he'd wait here to be collected. Nice and all as the old lady was, he didn't want to end up answering questions.

He had been dropped at this farmhouse just before dusk by Fr. Celsus. As far as the old couple were concerned, he was a Christian Brother. He had offered to pay the woman for his overnight lodging but she wouldn't accept anything. Jack wondered if the Volunteers would pay. He doubted it. After all, they'd say, there was a 'war' on and everyone had to do their bit. It was a cosy billet, just like the better rooming houses Percy had picked for them both when there wasn't a hotel nearby. But Percy never stayed anywhere more than once, especially in hotels. They were sure to be holding on to Percy's bounced cheques and had an eagle eye out for him.

With the window open, the sun shining in a cloudless sky and the only sounds those of birds singing, he lay on the bed and closed his eyes. And for a moment all was quiet. Just like the

99

momentary silence when the deafening hour-long shelling of the German frontline stopped, and all the singing birds within hearing burst into song. He remembered the day when everything changed for him.

A pale dawn sky gradually revealed itself through the lingering shell smoke drifting slowly to the north-east. Whistles blasted along the section of the front line trench jammed with soldiers of the King's Own Liverpool Rifles. NCOs herded men towards the ladders held against the trench's earthen wall.

'Over the top now, men.' Their platoon commander, a 2nd Lieutenant, just turned 19 and barely out of public school, urged them on despite the men's cumbersome full battle dress and the difficulty of climbing the steep ladder up onto no-man's-land. For Jack and Pat, a lad he had befriended on his arrival, their unacknowledged nerves fed into giddiness while waiting for their battalion's first time to go 'over the top.' They quietly mocked the few older fellows praying and sneered at the handful of malingerers slinking back to mingle with rear units. Those slackers would still have to go over the top, however much they delayed it. As each man stepped from the ladder onto the boot-churned mud, he followed those ahead who spread out, bayonets fixed, as they advanced. Pat was a few yards ahead. To Jack, it was like plodding through a ploughed field after two days of rain. Then, as the last of the thinning shell smoke drifted away, the rising sun broke through on the horizon. Its low rays shone directly into their eyes. Cap peaks down to shade the glare, the squaddies slowed, zigzagging around the shell holes and treacherous craters filled with filthy smelling water. They drew closer to their first barrier, German barbed wire. They were almost half way across no-man's-land. One man held the wire down while another clambered over it

– there were never enough wire cutters. Jack saw a soldier press his rifle muzzle against the top strand of barbed wire and fire. As the taut strand snapped, men on either side pulled it right back to its steel stave.

'Hold fire! No shooting without orders.'

Even as the NCO shouted, the dull metallic hammering of enemy machine guns began. Jack saw men dropping soundlessly across the ragged phalanx ahead.

'Advance, men. Be firm.'

The tone and accent announced the approach of the tall young lieutenant, his Webley pistol drawn. He strode ahead of them. Half a mile away, a sharp-eyed sniper from a Bavarian Alpine regiment scanned the line of advancing enemy soldiers with his telescopic sight. Spotting the subaltern's tell-tale Sam Brown officer's belt, he held his target in the cross-hairs for a second or two before squeezing the trigger. Seconds later the lieutenant fell backwards. Passing his still form, the two pals barely gave it a glance. Trudging through the mud constantly churned by unending mortar and artillery fire, Jack watched ahead for the shredded barbed wire, the jagged stave remnants, shattered rifle stocks, unexploded mortars and shells and all the other dangerous things waiting to catch the unwary.

'Are you all right there, Jack?' Pat shouted.

'Yes, Pat. But the mud is building up on me boots.'

'Well ...' Pat stopped, knees buckling and he fell back.

'Pat! Pat! Are you alright, mate?'

Jamming his rifle upright into the mud, Jack threw himself on his knees beside the still form. There was no sign of any bullet wounds on his body. Pushing Pat's peaked cap back, he saw the trickle of blood on his forehead. It didn't look a big enough wound to kill. Fumbling to remove the cap wasn't easy. Something was holding it back. Finally a hard tug did it. Then he wished he hadn't, on seeing the curved bloody skull shard and whitish grey matter in the cap. The heavy machine gun bullet had shattered the back of Pat's skull. In shocked calm, Jack took out his first aid kit. Removing a bandage, he began to bind Pat's head wound. He felt a blow on his shoulder and looked up. A sergeant had his Webley inches from Jack's face.

'Get up, soldier, and move on. The wounded will be looked after later.'

'He's my pal and he's badly wounded. I can't leave him here alone. Look, he's bleeding, sergeant.'

'I don't give a fuck if he's your pal. Or your brother. You're a fighting man, so fucking well get up and go kill a few Huns for your mate.'

'No. I'm waiting with him until the stretcher bearers come.'

Aiming the pistol at Jack's head, the sergeant spoke slowly. 'Listen, soldier, I am Battle Police. I'm going to count to three and if you haven't moved off by then, I'm going to shoot you dead.'

Jack continued his diligent bandaging of Joe's head, unmoved by the click of the Webley's safety catch.

'One, two ...' Pause. 'Three.'

Jack closed his eyes. Nothing happened.

'Fuck you, private.'

Holstering the gun, the sergeant hunkered down beside Jack. 'Gimme that,' he snarled. Taking the bandage from Jack's hand he expertly finished the job. 'If I was an officer you'd be fucking dead now. Shot for mutiny in the field of battle. Gimme your pay book and then get going. I'll deal with you later.'

'But Pat ... my pal ... who'll look after Pat?'

'Unless he sits up – and he won't –he'll be safe here until help comes for him and the rest of the wounded. There's nothing else you can do for your pal. So get moving or else ...!

A tap on the bedroom door brought Jack back to the present. The anxious voice of the farmer's wife said 'There's a young gentleman to see you, Brother.'

'I'll be down now, Mam.'

As he rose, the door opened and a lad of about seventeen barged in.

'I'm so sorry, Brother, I ...' The landlady quavered.

'That's alright, Ma'am, we've things to talk about. Don't you be worrying yourself.'

Even before the door was fully shut the young fellow blurted out 'I'm Stephen Hayes, eh ... Brother. Can you drive a tourer?'

'Yes.'

'Great! I've a trap outside. C'mon. Hurry. And don't forget

your bag.'

'What's the rush? The train isn't for another hour.'

'Forget about the train. I was told to tell you it's urgent Volunteer business.'

Sitting sideways in the trap, his legs anchoring his bag, Jack admired the easy way the lad managed the pony at a pretty smart pace.

'I'm Jack, Stephen.'

'And I'm Steve. How are yeh, Jack? Or is it Brother Jack?'

Jack smiled. 'That's for me to know and for you to find out. You're good at handling a pony and trap.'

'I've been working around horses since I was fourteen. And you get to know a horse. Dolly's great, not a bit vicious. And she always keeps her hooves to herself when you're beside her.

'Can you drive a motorcar?'

'I wouldn't know where to begin.'

'But there's those tractor motor things for pulling ploughs now, isn't there?' Jack asked.

Steve laughed. 'For gentry farmers, you mean?'

'What happened the man who was supposed to be driving the tourer? Couldn't he drive it?'

'Oh, yeah. Of course he could. He was Lord Cloncurry's driver before his lordship went bad. Anyway he woke up this morning very sick and has been vomiting since. So he's no use to us today.'

'There's got to be someone else in the town able to drive a tourer?'

'There might be but there's no need to look now that we've found you. And as we're late enough ... Jack! The Brother's collar ...you can't drive a tourer with that on!'

Feeling foolish, Jack detached the collar from its studs. 'If you stop the trap I'll open the bag and get me ordinary collar and necktie out.'

'Can't stop, Jack. Wait till we get to where we're going.'

After another ten minutes of side roads, Steve reined the horse back to a walk approaching an open farm gate. Turning in, he kept the pony at a slow trot down a long straight gravel drive between tilled fields ending at a big house surrounded by trees. He drove the trap around the side of the building. A high wall stretched back about fifty yards from the house with an archway half-way down. Slowing to walking pace, Steve took the trap under the arch and into a wide inner yard and stopped. Looking about, Jack saw a cobblestoned area bounded on three sides by a hay barn, a byre and stables. The empty tourer waited in the centre. Nearby, three smartly dressed young men stood smoking as they watched Jack and Steve approach. Jack recognised two of them as the pair who had dragged Bell from his tram seat. All three of them had a hand in their overcoat pockets. Dressed for the city, they looked completely out of place here. No one else was about.

'Stay here, Jack, and get your collar and tie back on while I tether Dolly. I'll explain to the lads why you're here.'

By the time Steve returned, Jack was wearing his regular collar, his tie in place and holding his bag.

'Put that back in the trap, Jack. It'll be looked after here. The lads told me I'm to sit beside you and give directions to town. So you get in the driving seat. You know how to get it started, don't you?'

'Yeah, of course.' Jack settled himself behind the tourer's wide steering wheel. When two attempts to start its engine failed, he stopped trying. He'd flood the engine if he kept that up. He put the gears in neutral and hauled on the handbrake. Time to have a go at the starting handle. Going to the front, he saw that was already in the engine. He got a good grip on it and turned it once slowly to get things inside moving a bit. Then with the handle grip in the bottom position, he jerked it upwards with all the strength he could muster. The noise of a top class engine coming to life and then running smoothly was satisfying. The three townies piled into the back passenger seat. Steve sat beside Jack.

'Where do I go, Steve?'

'Once outside this place turn right and I'll tell you from there.'

Twenty minutes later, they passed a railway station on the outskirts of a town. About a hundred yards on, Jack was directed to stop the car beside the footpath but to leave the engine running. There wasn't a soul in sight. As instructed, he stood on the road beside the engine, the bonnet propped up. Steve fiddled with the belts securing the spare wheel at the back. Jack, his head half turned, tapped the engine block with a spanner now and then as if he was working on it. The three passengers lounged at the front of the tourer.

Several minutes later, a man came around a corner from the town, an open newspaper in his hands. He glanced at them without interest and returned his gaze to the paper as he approached the car. Jack lightly tapped the engine block twice to let Steve know things were about to happen. He glanced quickly to the right. Though the man was coming closer, there was no sound of footsteps. So, Jack reflected, he had rubber soles and heels – the shoes of a detective. With his head bent, he tapped the engine block again. As the man passed, the only sounds were the rustle of his newspaper and the chat of the lads. Looking after him, Jack saw a tall, trim well-built man in a neatly fitting suit. His dark hair was cut short. He looked between thirty and forty years of age. A sudden fusillade of shots made Jack start. Three of the men were now on the footpath behind their target, guns drawn. Jack closed the bonnet. The man was staggering – he'd been hit bad – and trying to take something from his pocket. Two more shots felled him. A gust of wind blew open his newspaper. One of the fellas went to finish him off – *koo de grass* Percy said the French called it. As Jack revved the engine, the noise drowned the finishing shot. The three men swung themselves into the rear of the car. Steve slid into the passenger seat, his cap pulled well down and one hand half covering his face. The trio's leader spoke in a distinct Dublin accent. 'Let's get outa here, driver.' As they drove away, Jack brooded. Why hadn't the local Volunteers done this job?

ooooo0000ooooo

107

Marlborough Barracks, Dublin

Waite fidgeted on the upper deck of the tram to the Phoenix Park. His brief note from Cromie, unsigned and with no address, simply stated date, time and the venue - the Gresham Hotel. This, Waite knew, meant that their meeting in Dublin would be a day earlier, but in Marlborough Barracks. He had checked his Dublin street map before leaving his lodgings. It seemed the Barracks was an easy canter from the Vice Regal Lodge in Phoenix Park, and within a half hour's walk of Sackville Street. He would be lucky to be on time. As the tram reached Marlborough Road, he descended the stairs, crossed the road and ran.

'Good morning, Waite.' Cromie beamed over his glasses as Waite tried to control his breathing. 'We seem to have a really promising 'find' in your Jack. One or other of his informants seems to have gotten far closer to the top Shinners than your other informants.'

Waite strove to remain impassive.

'McKeever's information is rather thin on fact but fat on gossip. That sort of stuff sometimes confirms information we have from other sources. But now back to Jack's latest haul. It isn't – how shall I put it – earth-shaking, but it has promise.'

'I'm glad to hear that, Sir. I must confess I was becoming somewhat concerned.'

'Of course you were. You had no way of knowing the value of the information he has been sending us. So now let me tell you what we have gotten our hands on, thanks to him.' He picked up a folded sheet of paper from the desk. 'Firstly, we have eleven Sinn Féin Volunteers behind bars and facing a minimum of two years each.'

'Eleven! Really?'

'Don't get excited, Waite,' he said drily. 'There's a further 100,000 or so yet to be rounded up. As regards the weapons and explosives that we have seized, they are as follows: two shotguns, one Steyr automatic pistol, calibre 3.57 inch. And finally a single six inch shell. Not an arsenal, of course, but a promising start. As regards the shotguns, well, they're not Purdeys, need I say. Though quite useless in the field with their barrels cut short, they still have an advantage in close combat. But for all that, a two chamber carbine is no match for a hand-gun holding six to eight bullets.' He paused. 'Ah! Yes, the Steyr automatic pistol. Other than its empty magazine, it is in perfect condition. Unauthorised persons in the United Kingdom wouldn't find it easy to get their hands on the exact calibre bullets required for that and other Continental handguns. And that, thankfully, is a problem for the Shinners. Nevertheless, as all hand guns are feared at close range, how is one to know that the gun pointing at one is or isn't loaded? Finally, the 6 inch shell was very much a 'live' round, but as the Shinners have no artillery, it is of little use to them. However, it might well have been used as part of an improvised mine – assuming they had the correct fuse. Anyway I expect that the shell has been destroyed by our Ordnance chaps. So what's next? Yes, documents seized. Nothing much really. One of our old military instruction books – a pocket size *Field Exercises for Infantry* dated 1862. I can't see that being much help to Shinners skulking in woods and hills.' Pausing, he opened a manila folder on the desk and removed a small folded two-page newsprint sheet and held it up. 'Last but by no means the least is this, one of 135 copies of the Thuglock which we also seized.'

'Beg pardon, Sir?'

'It's spelled as you can see *An tOghlach* – that's old Irish script, I'm told, which means warrior or soldier or the like. But enough of all that now, Waite. Although Jack's stuff is promising, what we really need is hard information that will put us on the trail of their two top terrorists, Mulcahy and Collins.'

'I think you mentioned that pair before, Sir. Is Mulcahy still their so-called Volunteer Chief-of-Staff and Collins its Adjutant General?'

'Yes. But Collins is also Director of Intelligence – and I might add ...' he laughed. '... he is also the Minister of Finance in the outlawed talk-shop of the Dawl Erin upstart parliament. And, yes, both those self-styled generals remain firmly in the saddle and so are top of the list for bagging – preferably dead. No less important is anything that enables us to get our hands on the Shinners' war chest. We know that is well over £300,000.'

Waite gasped. 'What an enormous sum of money! How on earth did they get their hands on that?'

'It was collected – or rather extorted – throughout Ireland under the guise of the so-called Dawl Erin National Loan and lies concealed in hundreds of fake bank accounts throughout Ireland. That, Waite, is the money Police Magistrate Alan Bell was closing in on before he was dragged from his tram seat and murdered in cold blood. If – no, when – we get our hands on the Shinners' cash, and on the printing presses of both the Thuglock and the *Irish Bulletin*, the whole rotten Sinn Féin

110

house of cards will collapse.'

'The *Irish Bulletin*? I haven't seen that yet, Sir.'

'You are never likely to see it in a newsagent's shop. It is a proscribed publication,' Cromie said curtly. 'It is a very clever 'cut and paste' job of biased news made up of quotations of any and every report in Irish, British and foreign newspapers which could be damaging to the reputation of both the British Government and Crown Forces as regards Irish matters.'

'But if it is not on sale ...?'

'It is rather cunningly sent in the post in plain envelopes, personally addressed to each Member of Parliament and to the editors of newspapers and news sheets sympathetic to Ireland. It is also distributed in Paris to the international press there covering the Versailles negotiations.' He paused, frowning in thought. 'The signs are that this twisted propaganda is gradually gaining ground. It's imperative that we do something drastic to halt it. Get Jack to redouble his efforts on anything that will give us the whereabouts of Mulcahy and Collins.'

Thirty minutes later Waite was on the tram returning to the city centre.

oooooO000Oooooo

Waite glanced at his watch. He had been standing for fifteen minutes at the corner of Chatham St. and Grafton St., waiting for Kate. He spotted her approaching along the thronged pavement. Her face lit up in a smile as she saw him.

111

'Oh Stephen, I do apologise for being late but at the last minute Father asked me to collect a medical thermometer from Fannin's and I couldn't believe there were so many there waiting to be served. Anyway I'm here now.'

He smiled down at her. 'And that's what matters, Kate! Coffee? Where shall we go?'

'How about the Café Cairo? It's just across the street.'

Once seated and waiting to order, Waite asked 'You know, Kate, I am rather curious as to why it is named the Cafe Cairo? Is it because it is almost cheek by jowl with Tangier Lane – you know, to emphasize an Arabian theme? Or perhaps the proprietor is Egyptian?'

'Nothing as exotic as that, Stephen,' Kate said.

She discreetly motioned to a lady standing by a table in conversation with a diner.

'That lady standing over there, Stephen, is Mrs. Anne Lynch, the proprietress.'

'Isn't it unusual to have a lady owner?'

'Not anymore, and certainly not in Dublin. For instance, the Russell Hotel and restaurant is owned and managed by Lady Russell herself. And an extremely astute lady set up and runs The Monument Creamery shop and cafe further down Grafton street. Many businesses in Dublin are run by women.' There was a touch of asperity in her voice.

'Well, Kate, that just goes to show how out of touch I am.' Waite hastened to mend his fences. "But then, it shouldn't be a surprise. Ladies do have the vote now.'

'I don't, Stephen!' Waite thought he detected a light of battle in those hazel eyes.

'You don't? Why is that?'

'It seems that though Mr. Lloyd George considers me a competent woman – when I am qualified – to represent anybody in court as either a barrister or a solicitor, I am deemed too immature to vote until I reach thirty years of age!'

'Oh!' Waite paused, uncertain what to say about this ... this, yes, this discrimination. 'There is an awful lot I don't know about what went on in England when I was in Mesopotamia and Egypt,' he went on apologetically. 'We rarely saw British newspapers and even those were months out of date. And though we did get news of some major events, we never got any details. A good example of that were the details of the franchise extending to women.'

'Yes, well I can understand that, Stephen.' She patted his hand.

A waitress arrived to take their orders. It seemed to Waite that the conversation had entered a cul de sac. He glanced around.

'Do I see a piano over there?'

'It is indeed. Most afternoons, this is a *Café Dansant.*"

'Yes, I do recall some officers speak of them as quite acceptable places to meet respectable young ladies.'

'Without a Mama hovering in the wings?' Kate smiled.

'Yes. They did say the *Thé Dansants* were something like that. What exactly happens at one of these *Thé Dansants?*' Waite went on.

She grinned. 'One drinks tea, Stephen. And one dances.'

'And as a *Thé* is held only in the afternoon, those patronising the establishment ought by definition to be young persons of some leisure?'

'So it seems, Stephen, though I have no experience of it.'

'Oh.' Was Kate hinting she would like to attend a *Thé Dansant?* Would he now have the embarrassment of disclosing that he was a stranger to dance floors? And worse, that he was actually attending Senor Basagni's Academy?

His slight frown alarmed Kate.

'You see, Stephen, being a legal assistant in a busy solicitor's office for six and a half days every week hardly gives one any time to dance or drink tea in the afternoon. It would not be normal,' she went on 'for a young lady to visit a *Thé* alone. They normally attend in pairs or with an older companion. So despite the emancipation of women – which I embrace – that boundary between liberty and laxity nevertheless remains.' On hearing herself spout such pompous nonsense, Kate feared Stephen might now regard her as a prim Victorian governess.

'Your coffee, Miss.' Thank goodness! A diversion.

'And yours, Sir.'

As the waitress set down the gleaming silver pot, Kate knew she could not very well tell Stephen – of all people – that both the Cairo and Bonne Bouche premises were usually out of bounds to her because of her confidential work. It was a problem encountered by many young woman engaged in clandestine

114

work for Dáil Éireann. One could hardly spurn attractive young British Army officers by revealing one's Nationalist beliefs. On the other hand, a chilly response might well be regarded as a challenge. And worse, being pursued by some besotted subaltern might well lead to all sorts of complications, not least being the unwelcome interest of some zealous young Volunteer.

Kate decided to change the subject. 'Now, about our trip to Bellewstown Races later this week.'

'It was kind of your father to invite me.' He paused. 'Though I rather think you had a hand in that?'

'How could you think of such a thing of me?' She gave him a sidelong, mischievous glance.

'You know, Kate, before I met him I assumed both your parents were Irish. But he is English. Where did they meet?'

'In London, actually. You see, Grandfather – my Mother's father – was politically allied with Parnell in some way. So when Parliament sat he would stay in the Liberal Club there. And that is where my Mother and Father first met. His family had been Liberal supporters for years and were steadfast believers in Gladstone's Irish policy. Mother told me that theirs was a whirlwind romance. I rather think Father approves of you!' she confided.

'Oh, I am so glad to hear that!'

'I think, perhaps, Stephen, Father probably feels you may feel a little isolated. You know, without family or friends around, especially as you work alone.'

Whatever did Kate mean?

'Work alone? Not really. I meet business people most days now.'

'Of course, but what I mean is that you have no colleagues, no companions at work with you.'

'Well, yes, that's true. But then I have no experience of working with other people. So what you don't know, you don't miss.'

'Anyway, Stephen, let us get back to the arrangements for tomorrow. We'll travel to Bellewstown in Father's motor-car in the company of an old friend of his from their student days who is on a brief visit to Dublin. Colonel Benson is a charming man and very good company.'

The mention of so senior an officer troubled Waite. Would this 'friend' ask searching questions as to his War service and disdain his field commission?'

'I had no idea your father had been an Army man,' he said cautiously.

'He was never in the Army, Stephen.'

Waite paused and, in what he hoped was a tone of mild indifference, asked 'And what is Colonel Benson's regiment?'

'I really don't know. Does the Royal Army Medical Corps have regiments? Anyway, I can tell you he is one of its most senior surgeons. Father and he were at medical college together.'

Relieved, Waite continued on a lighter note. 'It will be most interesting to meet him. I have no memory at all of my one encounter with a military surgeon in the War.'

Kate's eyes widened. 'You never mentioned that to me, Stephen. What happened?'

'I had been put to sleep with gas in the Étaples Field Hospital just before the surgeon came into the operating theatre. When I awoke later in the ward, he visited me. But I was still too groggy from the gas to remember his face. And I never knew his name. Anyway my wound wasn't that complicated.'

'Oh! You were wounded, Stephen?' Her eyes were pools of concern, and Waite luxuriated in her attention.

'It was a simple flesh wound – nothing compared with what very many others experienced. Getting back to our trip to Bellewstown, will your Father be driving?'

'Goodness, no!' Kate laughed. 'Mama has forbidden him to drive as he never quite mastered the controls. We have George – a former Army driver – as our chauffeur.'

'And your mother, will she be there also?'

'Oh, no! She has never visited a racecourse since the War's end.' She would not embarrass Stephen by mentioning Mama's continuing grief for Tom, her second child and only son. He had succumbed to influenza two months following the Armistice.

Sensing a reserve on Kate's part, Waite decided to change the subject.

'So then, Kate, when and where on Friday shall I meet up with the Swanton racing party?'

117

'Between half past ten and eleven o'clock on Friday morning at St. Stephen's Green, directly opposite the Shelbourne Hotel.' Kate gathered up her gloves and handbag.

'Splendid! I look forward to my first ever visit to a racecourse.'

ooooo0000ooooo

Whitehall

Albert was looking uncharacteristically sombre as he joined Clive in his club. 'That chap Toplis we spoke about is dead.'

'How did that happen?' Clive grunted. 'Were you able to connect him to the thefts?''

'Yes. After our meeting, all barracks and base O.C.s were ordered to report any Toplis type of theft immediately to the Provost Marshall. All army installations within a fifty mile radius were alerted to ensure utmost vigilance by military police. The chief constable in each area was kept informed and agreed to have their detectives cooperating with those from neighbouring constabularies if required.'

'The net was closing, what?' Clive commented.

'Indeed,' Albert agreed. 'He was cornered and he shot and killed a taxi driver. A coroner's jury found him guilty of murder.'

'What was his background?'

'He joined the Royal Army Medical Corps in 1915. He was recorded as a front line stretcher-bearer in the initial stages of the Loos offensive. Then he was reported missing, whereabouts unknown. He next appeared in his home town as a decorated captain, no less, in officer's dress, Sam Brown belt, holster and pistol – and sporting a spurious wound stripe'. Albert filled his pipe. 'After his death, medals for valour, wound and campaign stripes, private effects belonging to other men, watches, cuff links, calling cards and even cheque books were found in his room.'

'I think I can see where this is going,' Clive said. 'As a stretcher-bearer, he would have been on the spot when the battle wounded were taken to the field hospitals.

'Indeed,' Albert agreed.

'And when those at death's door succumbed to their injuries, they were prepared for burial in temporary cemeteries and ... robbed of anything of value by despicable rogues such as Toplis.'

'Exactly,' Albert said heavily. 'And then, he simply re-enlisted in the RAMC under another name and reappeared at Étaples in 1917, where he was one of the instigators of the only mutiny in the history of the Army.'

'But the mutiny was suppressed.' Clive said. 'Why was he not arrested with the others?'

'He had vanished. Mind you, after rewards were posted for any information leading to his capture, he was arrested, along with an accomplice. The pair of them escaped one night by simply digging out the sandy soil under the wire. Toplis swam across the estuary and – disappeared. We can only assume he returned to England by bribing seamen on merchant ships to let him on board.'

Clive slumped in his seat. 'So this leaves things in the air. I had hoped to provide Sir Henry with more concrete evidence of the man's guilt – and some clue as to who his accomplices were.'

Albert brightened. 'As regards that, Clive, there is some good news. After the inquest, the police released Toplis's personal effects to his mother. All stolen Army and related property remain in Army custody, of course.'

'And the good news?'

'There was a photograph. Toplis sitting in an open tourer. Here it is.'

Clive studied it. 'He was a Major then, I see. One wouldn't doubt his spurious officer status if one didn't know better. And the tourer?'

'Stolen, of course.' He went on. 'Do you note anything else, Clive?'

'The driver. A private,' Clive exclaimed.

'And at the back of the photograph are two sets of initials,' Albert went on. 'P.H.T. – Toplis, obviously, and F.X.B. – the driver and partner in crime.'

Clive sat upright. 'Find him, Albert. Find that private. We'll pull some good out of this yet!'

Chapter 5

'...you do not declare war against rebels.'

Lloyd George, Minute sheet on Ireland,

' note of conversation' 30 April 1920, Cab.23/21

Jack sat on the higher end seat of the packed charabanc. The man he was following - Jack decided to call him Eddie - was clearly in view sitting in the second row seat. The passengers, all men, were bound for the Bellewstown Races. Two days previously, he had been told that a senior Volunteer officer – a Commandant - from the midlands would be coming to Dublin on Volunteer business that evening. A Cumann na mBan lady would identify him to Jack. Jack was to keep his distance while following him wherever he went.

A burly man wearing a grey trilby stepped off the train at Broadstone station. The lady who alighted a few yards behind him caught Jack's eye and inclined her head towards the departing passenger. She walked in the opposite direction. Following Eddie outside, Jack saw him hail a horse cab back towards the city centre. Jack followed on foot, confident that he would be able to keep pace with the cab in the heavy traffic. The cab went along Western Way down past the Black Church to Parnell Square and then continued to Mountjoy Square where it turned right into Gardiner Street. A hundred or so yards behind, Jack saw it stop. As he drew closer he saw the sign for Lynch's Hotel. Eddie paid off his cab and went inside. After an hour, Jack concluded that Eddie had booked in for the night. He reported back to Staunton who told him Eddie would be at the Gresham Hotel the next morning for a meeting on Volunteer matters and that Jack was to continue following him wherever he went afterwards.

Jack didn't need Mr Staunton to tell him that a man in a senior position could do a lot of damage, not only to the Volunteers, but to the 'Organisation'. But that was someone else's problem. His job was to keep an eye on everything Eddie did and who he met.

Well before 9 a.m. the following morning, Jack watched the main door of the Gresham Hotel across the width of Sackville Street. Eddie strolled along at about 10 a.m. When he emerged about three quarters of an hour later, Jack followed him. To Jack's frustration, Eddie spent the day between the Kildare Street Museum and the Animal Museum, full of dead animals and birds. He spoke to no-one. By five o'clock, Jack had had his fill of ancient artifacts and stuffed animals and had worked his way through two newspapers, down to the smallest advertisement. Eventually, Eddie returned to his hotel. By eight o'clock, Jack decided that Eddie was in for the night. Ravenous, Jack went to a cafe and had a double fish and chips and tea before reporting back to Staunton who told Jack to keep tailing Eddie wherever he went the next day.

Jack was outside Eddie's hotel at half past eight the following morning. Eddie came out without his travelling bag just after nine. Following him to Sackville Street, he saw him turn into Abbey Street. Quickening his pace, Jack stopped at the corner and glanced around. Eddie was at the end of a short queue on the pavement alongside a charabanc directly outside Wynn's Hotel. Jack zigzagged back through the slower horse drawn vehicles to the other pavement. Ambling towards the charabanc, he saw a large white sign resting on the folded hood. It offered a day return trip to the Bellewstown Race meeting for two shillings. Jack guessed Bellewstown must be fairly close to Dublin. Well, as his orders were to follow Eddie everywhere, the Shinners would be paying for this trip.

Joining the queue, Jack moved gradually along until it was his turn to pay the required two shillings, a stiff sum that, but one that kept rowdies and bowsies away. Directed to the higher rows at the back, he shared a seat with four other race goers.

Absorbed in predicting likely winners, they took no notice of him. Jack saw that Eddie was four rows ahead. About ten minutes later, the charabanc was full. Before moving off the driver turned to his passengers. 'Quiet, gentlemen, please,' he shouted. 'We're leaving now and we'll only be stopping at Balbriggan for those of you who want to have a snack or a drink. And after that I won't be stopping for anyone who needs to stop before we reach the racecourse.' He grinned. 'You have been warned!' He started the engine. The vehicle lumbered slowly away from the pavement and out on the roadway.

Though it was Jack's first time in a charabanc, it was, in his view, nothing but a stretched out motor car with, he guessed, the engine of a lorry. With a retractable hood, it would be an omnibus. Just as well the weather was fine and dry. He had a good view as they passed the ruins of the General Post Office, gutted by shellfire in the Rebellion. Well, with a H.Q. in the centre of a city what else did the rebels expect? Fifteen minutes later, they began the long uphill drive to Santry, the engine roaring. The road levelled out for a while as they passed what someone called Santry Demesne. From then on they were on the open plain of north county Dublin.

The familiar engine noises recalled memories of his short 'service' as 'Army' driver for the 'Colonel' or the 'Major' or whatever officer Percy happened to be at the time. Percy didn't talk much when Jack was driving. But he certainly did when he had a few drinks taken – he always forgot Jack didn't drink. So he had learned a lot from Percy. Yeah, quite a few tricks about how to get along. He also learned a lot about people. About the things they got up – the bad things mostly, but other things too that were useful to know. Percy should have taken his own advice. The last thing Jack had expected was for Percy to be shot dead. On reflection, though, that wasn't too surprising. After some months with that trickster he had had a feeling it was time to get away from him altogether. He had been right.

Approaching the turn-off road to Bellewstown, the charabanc stopped behind a line of waiting motor cars. A few seats in front, a man stood up to view the road ahead. 'There's Shinners on the road stopping the traffic,' he shouted. Jack was astonished that the Volunteers would attempt any public action with so much traffic around.

'Have they guns?' a voice asked.

'No. But they're all dressed up in their Sunday best and ... yeah, they're wearing white armbands.'

Another voice. 'It looks like they're holding back the traffic that's coming the other way as well.' There was a puzzled silence as the passengers craned their necks for a view.

'It's O.K. now,' the first man said. 'They're letting motors on the other side turn into the side road to Bellewstown first. Then I think it's our turn.'

The standing observer spoke again. 'The armbands have INV on them.'

Jack couldn't believe what he was hearing. INV – Irish National Volunteers – showing themselves in public! One of the fellows beside him spoke out.

'INV? Ah! The Invincibles are back!' General laughter was followed by a further quip. 'The driver wouldn't be Skin the Goat, would he?'

A single titter faltered in a stony silence. Jack didn't understand.

He must ask Mr. Staunton what the Invincibles are and who is this Skin the Goat fella. As the charabanc began to inch forward, the first voice spoke again. 'Yeah, they are Sinn Féin Volunteers. The question now is, what's the Constabulary doing?'

'Safe in their Balbriggan barracks, I'd say.'

An uneasy silence followed this outright Republican sentiment. Jack well knew that these days some things were best left unspoken in public – no matter what side you were on.

Progress was slow on the rising side road to Bellewstown. The charabanc finally reached the plateau of the racecourse. They passed the fenced-off area of the Enclosure. The back of its small viewing stand was just inside the timber palisade. About a hundred yards further on the charabanc turned into a field where motor vehicles were parked. Their driver stood up and announced the exact time he would be leaving. 'And if any of youse are not here then, I'm not waiting. It'll be shank's mare back to Dublin for you.'

Jack was one of the first off. As he waited for Eddie to alight, he looked around casually. On the other side of the road, a wide grass verge was thronged with people. Through some gaps in the crowd, he saw the timber rail that separated the race goers from the horses thundering by. For those alongside the rail there was a free view of the finish line. Turning, he saw Eddie leave the field and head for the enclosure. With so many people about, following him was easy. Looking back as he crossed the road, Jack could see the top of a fair ground tent in the distance. As he passed the small church and school he had seen from the charabanc, he had a closer look at a row of thatched cottages next to a packed pub at the corner of a small

126

country lane. Drinkers stood along the pub front and down the lane. And that was all there was to Bellewstown. Why was it called 'town' when it wasn't even a village! There were no bookies' stands there, so anyone taking bets outside here would be a chancer. And that's when the unwary lost money on winners as the 'bookies' were never around for the pay-out. On the track side, the open grassy area ended at a wooden picket fence at least six feet high which blocked off the enclosure from the road. A short distance behind that was the back of the racing Stand. Some fellows on the charabanc had joked about reserving a place on that but everyone knew it was just for owners, trainers, and those with deep pockets. Inside would be the licensed bookies from Dublin, Drogheda and Dundalk, each with their own 'stands.'

Jack was now a couple of yards behind Eddie in the short queue a couple of yards from the timber entrance door in the fence, his three penny piece entry fee ready.

Inside, he thought he had lost Eddie, then he picked out the grey trilby about twenty yards further on. He was buying a race card. As he hadn't expected it to be so crowded in here, Jack knew he'd have to keep a sharp eye on him or he'd lose sight of him. It puzzled him that the Commandant would bother coming to an out-of-the way racecourse like this. After all, there were at least three first class racecourses in Dublin – Phoenix Park, Leopardstown and Baldoyle. Was Eddie meeting someone special here? Someone he couldn't risk being seen with in Dublin? Someone from outside Dublin? Yeah, people came to the city from all over the country every day. But you wouldn't waste a day coming all the way from the country to Dublin just to go to Bellewstown. Well, that is, unless you were gentry or well-off enough to own a motor car. Nearly all the

fellas on Jack's charabanc had Dublin accents. The few that
didn't had English ones. Off-duty officers? Volunteers? There
was nothing unusual about that. Would there be any
Volunteers from Eddie's own Brigade here? Did it matter? He
didn't know any of them so none of them would know him. All
the same, Jack resolved to keep his wits about him from now
on. Just in case.

ooooo0000ooooo

Normal conversation, Kate thought, was always difficult in fast-
moving open motor cars. Father's pre-War model, though
slower, had the added nuisance of a very noisy engine.
Thankfully, these days they rarely travelled long journeys as a
family. The Curragh, Punchestown and, as today, the
Bellewstown races, were the outer limits. There was another
disincentive to driving in the wider countryside – one risked the
possibility of a motor car being commandeered by the
Volunteers – or seized by the Sinn Féiners, according to one's
point of view. Though today was not sunny, it was still dry and
warm with only a mild breeze – when stationary. Thankfully,
her driving veil resisted sudden gusts of wind. She felt rather
sorry for Stephen who shared the front seat, and the brunt of
the wind, with the chauffeur, although the latter was buttoned
up in a leather coat, with elbow length leather gauntlets and
driving goggles.

She marvelled that Stephen had never been at a race meeting,
though it was understandable considering that his public school

128

years had been spent either in England during term time or back home in Simla for the holidays. He had been curious for some reason on learning that his fellow guest at Bellewstown would be an army colonel, and then appeared relieved on learning that he was Medical Corps. Kate frowned slightly. It was a puzzle, she decided, but perhaps she was imagining things.

For his part, Waite resolved never again to be misled by glamorous magazine photographs of chic young people sitting happily in tourers as they were driven along under blue skies. He had thought his woollen coat would withstand the elements, but it was proving inadequate. Notwithstanding the half-windscreen, the front seat passenger and driver acted as a partial windbreak for those behind. Still, he thought, beggars can't be choosers and he really shouldn't indulge in self-pity. He was the guest of thoroughly nice people who had welcomed him into their home. Of course, Kate must have spoken well of him ... enthusiastically, perhaps? And being a fellow Englishman of her father probably helped. Yet, what a rotter he was, continuing to pose as Stephen Lexington. Feeling thoroughly guilty, he turned to look back at Kate who sat between her father and the RAMC Colonel. She seemed pensive, but then their eyes met and her face lit up in a radiant smile. For him. He still couldn't believe that such a beautiful woman actually liked him – maybe actually ... might come to love him? Aware that both older men were looking at him, he nodded an embarrassed half-smile.

ooooo0000ooooo

George brought the car to a halt at the short grass verge between the road and the fenced enclosure. Dr Swanton ushered his small party the few yards to the picket entrance. Inside, they followed him up the steps to the viewing stand which was almost full. Kate explained that most of the others on the stand were either owners or trainers, along with their guests.

Waite was impressed with the sweeping view of the course, almost entirely visible with the exception of the north-west turn in the track. There, a small gorse-covered rocky outcrop obscured the view of the runners until they came into view turning the last bend before the straight home.

'This is quite a magnificent view, Nigel,' the colonel said. 'What are those mountains?'

'They are the Mourne Mountains which, as the song goes, roll down to the sea. And before us are the plains of Meath.'

'Anybody interesting here?' the colonel looked around.

'Yes,' said Dr Swanton, 'that's young Saunderson up there – he's the Viceroy's personal secretary – to the right behind us. And beside him is Frank Brook who is a member of the Irish Privy Council and Chairman of the Great Eastern Railway Company. I rather think the tall gentlemen flanking both of them are RIC men in plain clothes. Armed too, I'd say.'

Kate bit back the information that Brook had just sacked 200 railway workers for refusing to run trains bearing armed soldiers or police. Such a turn in the conversation to the 'Troubles' would spoil the occasion for everyone.

She turned to Waite. 'Do you fancy a flutter, Stephen? I know

I would. It's your first race – you must mark the occasion.'

'I must confess I was waiting for the subject to arise,' the colonel interjected. 'Your first race, Mr Lexington? How can that possibly be?'

Waite explained that his public school days – devoid of any race-going experience – were barely two months over when the War broke out, and within weeks he, by then an insignificant second lieutenant, was on his way to France with one of the four Divisions of the Indian army.

'May I ask the name of your school, Mr. Lexington?' the Colonel asked.

'I was at Grove End, Colonel, Sir.'

'That's in Yorkshire, isn't it?'

'It is indeed, Colonel, Sir. Close to Richmond.'

Kate was mildly surprised at Stephen's deference to the Colonel. After all, he was no longer a serving officer. On the other hand, the habit of six years of Army discipline was probably ingrained and not easily shaken off.

'Just as I thought. I knew a good chap from near there. Weston. A superb surgeon, need I say. Did wonders with men in South Africa who were ... badly wounded.' He paused. 'Well, what about our bets?'

They picked their mounts and decided on their wagers.

'Which bookmaker would you recommend, Nigel?' the Colonel asked.

'Patsy Cadogan, of course. He has an instinct for form and the odds to match.' Dr Swanton laughed. 'Patsy was one of the first bookmakers in Dublin to acquire a telegraphic address. Naturally, he advertised it in the newspapers. A couple of days later, two gentlemen from Dublin Castle visited him,' he chuckled.

'Civil servants?'

'In a manner of speaking, Geoffrey, yes. They were Dublin Metropolitan Police detectives. They instructed Patsy to cease and desist from using *Cadogan, Dublin* as his telegraphic address.'

'Why so?' the Colonel asked.

'Because His Excellency Earl Cadogan , then Lord Lieutenant and Governor General of Ireland, had begun receiving ante-post bets by telegram at the Vice Regal Lodge in the Phoenix Park.'

Kate joined in he general laughter this anecdote always elicited despite having heard it many times.

'So now,' her father continued, 'as the next race is in 15 minutes time let us all write out our wagers. Perhaps then Mr Lexington might volunteer to place them with Patsy?'

'Really, Father! Mr Lexington is surely not to act as a bookie's runner on his first outing at a race!' Kate exclaimed.

Waite suppressed a smile. 'I look forward to the experience.'

ooooo0000ooooo

Drawing closer, Jack followed Eddie as he made his way to the line of bookmakers to the right of the Stand. Though more punters were concentrated there, most of them taller than him, Jack had no difficulty keeping him in sight. He relaxed as Eddie peered at the chalked odds on the little blackboards on the makeshift stands offered by each of the few bookies there. As Eddie joined the small queue before Sam Curley's stand, Jack glanced at his card. This, the 12 p.m. race was the first of the day – The Crockafotha Plate. With thirty runners, it was a big field for a one mile race, especially one on the flat. Only the first dozen horses off would have the advantage in a stampede of thirty nags. Now several paces behind Eddie, Jack saw Curley now and then glance towards the other bookies, watching out for any signal of heavy betting on one horse. Even as Jack watched with a connoisseur's eye, the bookie's finger wiped out a price and chalked in another in seconds – shortening the odds. Eddie was next to bet. Jack saw him hand over two one pound banknotes – nearly a week's pay for a skilled workman. Stuffing the notes into his pocket, the bookie repeated Eddie's selection to his clerk who then made rapid entries in 'The Book'. As the bookie finished scribbling out the booking slip, his clerk called out. 'No.135.' Jack memorised the number so that Staunton could check later with the bookie just how much Eddie had won or lost on this race.

Eddie moved away. A little further on there was some sort of commotion causing those just ahead to step back and block his way. Two fellows, both wearing white INV armbands, shoved their way through the throng, grasping a protesting youth between them as he insisted 'I didn't pick that oul fella's pocket. Honest to God.'

133

Waite handed his bet list and cash to Cadogan, a fit looking man in his seventies perched on an improvised stand, with a leather satchel on his hip. As he turned away, glancing at the small piece of paper he was given, all Waite could see was a handwritten number and the time of the race. This was an arcane business, he concluded. Threading his way through the crowd, he stopped in astonishment as two neatly dressed young fellows with smart flat caps crossed his path. They sported INV armbands. Where was the R.I.C.? What on earth was going on, with Sinn Féin rebels in their Sunday best strutting about in public at a race meeting? In seconds, they were out of sight. He had to admit that they bore no resemblance to the photographs of Fenian dynamitard ruffians or the murderous looking Invincibles shown him during training. He didn't think they were armed. Had any of the Swanton party seen them from the stand? Ought he mention what he had seen to Kate? Perhaps not. After all, to her he was a commercial insurance representative with no interest in politics, indeed, he had always represented himself as a neutral outsider as regards events in Ireland, though one who genuinely wished for the best peaceful outcome.

In the distance, he saw a photographer assembling a camera on a tripod on the grass in front of the Stand. Kate had been scanning the crowd looking for him. Colonel Benson distracted her.

'A photographer there, I see, Nigel. He's got one of those new big cameras.'

'I expect he's taking pictures for the next issue of the *Irish Field* – he was back last year for the first time since before the War. Perhaps we shall feature in the next issue,' Dr Swanton laughed.

'Well, if it is, Margery will be greatly pleased,' the colonel said, adjusting his hat to a new angle. 'It might even encourage her to accompany me on my next visit if she realises normal social life goes on here in spite of the Troubles.'

Waite rejoined the group and passed the betting slip to Kate's father as he exclaimed 'We are about to have our likeness took!'

'Really, Father, your Oirish brogue is nothing short of Boucicault!' Kate reproved.

'I say, Nigel, something's going on down there,' the colonel exclaimed, passing the field glasses to Dr Swanton.

A commotion higher up behind caught their attention. A voice called 'The Shinners are down there, towards the picket fence to the left!' The two men came into view, frog-marching a young man between them. As they disappeared from view beside the stand, speculation broke out.

'Nigel, what do the initials INV stand for?'

'They are the Irish National Volunteers,' Dr Swanton responded. 'They are from the same stable as the bounders who started the rebellion.'

A voice behind them exclaimed 'The military have arrived!'

About twenty soldiers, bayonets fixed, emerged from both sides of the stand and fanned out at the edge of the crowd. Their

O.C., accompanied by another smaller group of soldiers, marched into the multitude, which parted before them. Dr Swanton stood on tiptoe, but could not see what was going on. Comments flew.

'They've cornered the Shinners!'

'Where?'

'Close by the winning post rail.'

'But the horses will be going to the start for the next race!'

'Will there be shooting?'

'No! The horses would panic and the day will be ruined.'

'Look, the military have surrounded the Shinners.'

A disbelieving voice said 'They're talking, would you believe!'

After a pause, the voice said 'The military are leaving ... and the Shinners are still there!'

As the horses lined up for the start, attention became focussed on them, with all eyes on the highly-strung animals. The race was underway. Waite looked around. Everybody seemed totally concentrated on the race. He concluded that the Volunteer episode had somehow resolved itself.

ooooo0000ooooo

So the joker on the charabanc was right: the Volunteers were now doing a peeler's job catching robbers! Well that made a change from robbing anything they could get their hands on in and outside Birr Barracks! Jack realised he had lost sight of Eddie. He pushed harder through the crowd. To his relief, he spotted him making for the right hand side of the stand. Jack changed direction and made his way to the timber fence separating the public from the enclosure. It would be a good place to stand and watch the race course while keeping Eddie in sight. The grey fedora was bent over his race card. Suddenly there was a roar of approaching lorry engines. A platoon of armed soldiers with fixed bayonets ran around from the back of the stand, led by a full lieutenant. Jack glanced at Eddie as the soldiers passed by him. He didn't look a bit concerned, and him a Volunteer officer! Now he was looking at his watch as the soldiers followed their officer in to the crowd, pushing racegoers aside with their rifle butts.

oooooOOOOOooooo

The volume of noise rose with the excitement of the crowd as the skittish, prancing horses approached the starting line. Then they were off. Glancing back, Jack saw Eddie talking to a man. In brown tweed cap and jacket, knicker-bocker breeches and leggings, the fellow looked like a prosperous farmer. Yet, from the way he stood, there was a military cut to him. Eddie and he were talking together as though they knew each other well. Something changed hands, too quickly for Jack to spot what it was. Then the newcomer raised his hat in a polite farewell. Jack saw he had curly red hair. He walked back around the stand and out of sight. Jack was in a quandary. Who should he follow now? Eddie, he reasoned, would have to return to the charabanc if he was to get back to Dublin. That wouldn't be for a couple of hours yet. But this new fellow was interesting. Best follow him, Jack resolved, as Mr. Staunton would want as much information about him as Jack could get. Eddie was now walking back into the crowd. Jack moved quickly after the other man. The mounting excitement of the crowd grew as the first horses entered the final run to the post. Walking around the side of the stand he saw the newcomer had already gone out. As he approached the exit door, the roars of the crowd told him the first of the horses were fast approaching the finishing line. All attention would be on the nags now. There was no sign of the red-haired man behind the stand. He'd pick a good spot outside to watch and follow his man as far as possible.

Outside, three military lorries were stopped in line, partially blocking the road. A crowd had gathered around them. The soldiers ignored them.

About twenty yards back, Jack stopped to watch. The redheaded man was chatting with an Army officer. So Eddie's contact was in direct touch with the military. Mr Staunton would be interested to hear that. He then turned to point at something and Jack saw his face. Jack froze. It was the prosecutor at his court martial!

Chapter 6

'The more you shoot, the better I will like you, and I assure you that no policeman will get into trouble for shooting any man.'

Colonel G. F. Smyth, Divisional Commissioner RIC, Cork and Police Commissioner for Munster at RIC Barracks, Listowel, Co. Kerry, 19th June 1920.

'The good news, Waite, is that up to the end of August the Shinners believed they had complete run of the countryside, but that is no longer the case.' Cromie lolled in his chair in the empty officers' mess of Marlborough Barracks.

'Yes, it was beginning to look as if they had,' Waite agreed.

'And why were they were so cocky?' Cromie aimed his lit cigarette at Waite. 'Because until then the night foot patrols of the R.I.C. in the country areas were armed with single shot carbines, all very well for nabbing poachers and cattle thieves, but no match for ambushes by bands of well armed Shinners who hit-and-run and then vanish into the surrounding countryside. The lowest point was earlier this year when the Shinners began attacking the smaller, poorly fortified rural barracks. Dozens of them had to be evacuated and the Shinners promptly destroyed them.'

'Has anything changed since then?'

'I can tell you the tables are being turned on the Shinners by those splendid chaps of the Auxiliary Police Division, R.I.C. They have tourers fitted with machine guns and searchlights. Accompanied by Crossley tenders packed with constables armed to the teeth, they can cover wide stretches of countryside both day and night. Needless to say the Shinners give them a wide berth.'

'That's very encouraging, Sir. I had no idea the Auxiliaries were so well armed and organised.'

'Oh, yes. And with more and more reinforcements to come,' Cromie said complacently.

'Why are they called the Black and Tans?' Waite asked.

'Oh, some wag called them that and it stuck. But it is not said with the same affection they hold for the original Black and Tans.'

'Original ... I don't understand. Who were they?'

'They are a pack of hounds run by a long-established Limerick hunt on the border with Tipperary called the Scarteen Black and Tans.'

'Oh yes, of course!' Waite exclaimed as light dawned. 'The Auxiliary Division officers wear those black Glengarry-type bonnets with their Army dress.'

'Former officers', Waite. And without military insignia of rank and regiment. They are R.I.C. officers, not Army officers. And, need I say, temporary police officers at that.'

'Indeed, Sir,' Waite said stiffly. Cromie's clarification was both unnecessary and irritating, given his own 'temporary' status. 'But why do they wear that mixed uniform of police tunic and khaki trousers or vice versa?'

'Well, at the outset the R.I.C. did not have sufficient stocks of uniforms for the sudden increase in constables. They were forced to improvise. But the important thing is they are far better armed than the R.I.C. ever was. Furthermore, as ex-soldiers they know how to handle weapons and can give as good as they get.' He paused, yawning. 'Anyway, to business. Jack. I'm glad to tell you that his stuff has improved by leaps and bounds, even though he has still had no success as regards the whereabouts of Mulcahy and Collins. We also need anything that will enable us get our hands on the printing presses of the *Irish Bulletin* and *An tOglach* .' He paused. 'Not forgetting the secret offices of Dawl Airun. And finally and

141

most importantly, I would like to know who Jack's contact is and how is that fellow getting this first class information.'

'Well, if the information is so good, why look a gift horse in the mouth, Sir?' Waite ventured.

'I'll tell you why. Jack is our only go-between linking this valuable information and its source. If anything happened to Jack, then that's an end to it. So I want you to put this to Jack: tell him you want to meet his source for that very reason. It can be anywhere – Dublin, Cork, Galway, Belfast or even London – and wherever you do meet, I guarantee there'll be nobody about who might pose a threat to his best informant.' He paused. 'And there will be a bonus for Jack.'

ooooo0000ooooo

As Clive walked down the corridor, Albert hailed him from the stairwell. 'I have news, Clive. Shall we go to your office?'

Clive sighed as he removed his topcoat. 'I hope it's good news, Albert. It's been a bad day.'

'We now know far more about the mystery man in the photograph, F.X.B. – to begin with, his name is Francis Xavier Booth.'

Clive settled into his chair. 'Xavier? What an odd name.'

'Francis Xavier is, I understand, an R.C. saint. Anyway, Booth was in the Liverpool Rifles. He is definitely not on our War Dead list. And it seems he has a wife and three children living in Liverpool.'

'Where is he?' Clive enquired.

'He is on the current list of Army deserters.'

'Ah, that does complicate matters.' He paused. 'Have we any idea as to when and where he deserted?'

'Yes, there's a letter on his regimental file from his wife to the War Office in August 1916.'

'That was the middle of the Somme Offensive,' Clive interjected. 'Go on. What did it say?'

'She wanted to know what had become of her husband and that she had not received a letter from him in weeks.'

'So the poor woman thought he was dead or missing?'

'Yes.'

'This fellow was a despicable scoundrel,' exclaimed Clive.

'I agree,' replied Albert. 'But only if our F.X.B. really was Booth.' He held the photograph so Clive could see it more clearly. 'Booth was born in 1890. Our photograph of F.X.B. with Toplis shows a man who is aged about 19 or 20. We have shown it to Mrs Booth and she is emphatic that F.X.B. is not her husband.'

'Ah,' Clive said heavily. 'We may conclude that Booth's remains lie in a military cemetery somewhere in France with the name and number of that man in the photograph over his grave. The driver in the photograph stole his name along with his army pay books and identity discs.'

'I believe that it most probably took place in a Casualty Clearing Station,' Albert went on. 'Or indeed in the morgue. Toplis was in the RAMC – we may assume his accomplice was with him there, and seized his opportunity.

Clive rose and picked up his overcoat. 'I'm glad you stopped me to give me this information, Albert. I shall be meeting Sir Henry in the morning and at least I can report real progress in this investigation. It would greatly please him if we could nail down this accomplice once and for all. Do please carry on.'

ooooo0000ooooo

Jack left the tram at the stop at Herbert Park in Ballsbridge. The park was one of the places Mr. Lexington had picked for emergency meetings. Near the pond, he said. As he had never been here before, Jack decided to have a quick look around the place – just as Percy would have done in case he had to scarper. With two hours to spare before their meeting, he had plenty of time. Turning into Herbert Road, he saw that the right side of the Park was mainly open green space, with trees and bushes at intervals. The other side was much the same except for an inner line of trees and shrubbery with meandering pathways stretching end to end.

Other than two white haired old men ambling along, no one else was about. As he approached the trees, he could hear the high-pitched voices of small children. Passing through the short curving pathway between trees and bushes, he reached a narrow river ... no, it was a long narrow pond that stretched away the length of the park to the right with pathways on both sides. Not far away there was a small playground where nannies tended to small children, a few of them wheeling perambulators. As he drew closer, he saw that all the children were dressed to the nines. No unwashed barefoot street urchins here! A few of the uniformed women held small dogs on a leash. At the edge of the pond on the opposite side a little girl – her nanny inches behind – threw bread scraps to ducks thrashing about in the water.

Walking the short distance back towards Ballsbridge, he saw an open gate there. Good! Another way out. Sauntering up the opposite path, he glanced around. Most of the nannies were giving their full attention to the children in their care. Here and there a few stood chatting in the shelter of the park's east wall. All of them kept an eye on the slightly older children playing together. Smiling inwardly, he watched four small children obediently march ahead of their nurse at a pace which he guessed was intended to tire them out.

It was quieter at the pond's upper end and he decided to sit on the bench there. Yeah, this was a good place to have a meeting. No Volunteer would dare hang about here with the Black and Tans billeted two minutes away at Beggars' Bush barracks. It suddenly struck him that all throughout the War, every day here was probably just like this, calm and peaceful with only the sounds of children playing. No-one here would have had any idea of what a battlefront or shell-levelled towns and villages looked like.

The screams of a child had him instantly on his feet. About thirty yards ahead, a little boy clung to his nanny. A few feet away, a half-grown Alsatian held a yelping Pekingese by the neck and was shaking it. Jack raced to the scene, grabbed the mongrel's tail with both hands and pulled upwards with all his strength. The cur twisted, releasing the tiny animal and squirmed, trying desperately to bite his attacker. Jack spun the animal around in a circle twice to keep the snapping jaws away. By the third spin, the animal's snarls had turned to yelps. Using all his strength in a final whirl, he let it go. Rising over the pond for a second or two, its legs thrashing uselessly in the air, the dog landed with an enormous splash in the middle. Quickly surfacing, it paddled like the hammers of hell and scrambled out onto the opposite path, shot away into the bushes and was gone.

Despite her shock, the nanny was making every effort to calm the child whose tear-filled eyes were fixed on the unmoving Pekingese. Without thinking, Jack picked up the little tyke, his hand under its chest. The body was warm but its heart wasn't thumping and there was no sign of blood. Yeah, dead as a door nail. He'd seen shock do that once or twice in the War when the blast of a nearby shell burst stopped a man's heart.

He heard himself tell the nanny that the animal was sleeping from the fright and that he would take it to an animal doctor. He didn't know what made him say that but it seemed to work as the little fellow's sobs quietened.

'Did you hear that, Desmond, this kind man is going to take Rover to the Cats' and Dogs' Home for a rest.'

Jack was impressed at how quickly the young woman had got over her shock and calmed down the little fellow. She really had a way with small kids. And she seemed to be a really nice person. He liked her. He wanted to know ... to meet her again. He would have only one chance.

'Look, Miss,' he winked at her. 'Why don't I take the little doggie to the Cats' and Dogs' Home right now?'

'Why?' the little fellow asked, as he wiped his tears dry on his sleeve.

'So the dog doctor can give him something to make him feel better.' Turning his head so that the child couldn't see him, Jack turned to the girl and mouthed 'It's d-e-a-d'. Her eyes widened and she smiled. 'Thank you very much, Sir. Please do that.'

Jack nodded violently. 'And, Miss, what's Rover's ... address? I'll call back later and tell you what the animal doctor said.'

'That's very good of you, Sir. It's 148 Fitzwilliam Square.' She hesitated, then went on, her words coming in a rush. 'Best come round to the Mews behind – the number is on the Mews door – and pull the bell there. That'll ring next to the kitchen. I'll be there in the mid-morning when the housekeeper is out shopping for cook and Desmond is having his nap. So maybe I could bring you into the kitchen for a cup of tea and you could tell me about the dog. The family will be very grateful to you.'

Jack was delighted. No one had ever talked to him like that. She was about his age with a lovely, friendly manner. Her brown hair peeped from under her straw bonnet and she had huge brown eyes. And she was so concerned about someone else's brat! Getting a hold of himself, he continued in what he hoped was a normal voice. 'O.K., Miss, I'll do that. And by the way I'm Jack ... Jack Kelly.'

'I'm Mabel Clancy – but May to my friends.'

'Right, Miss Clancy, I'll have to rush off now and get to the Cats & Dogs Home as soon as possible.'

'Oh, thank you very much, Mr. Kelly. And remember, it's 148 Fitzwilliam Square. And as I said, the number is on the back Mews.'

'I won't forget it, Miss.' He grinned and turned away. Walking through the short winding path through the trees and clumps of bushes, he flung the dead animal as far into the undergrowth as he could. Now for his meeting with Mr. Lexington.

ooooo0000ooooo

Grafton Street was thronged with shoppers. The two men joined the crowd as they turned into Suffolk Street. Liam Tobin put a detaining hand on Collins's arm. 'There he is, Mick.'

'So that's him outside Mitchell's with the newspaper?'

'Yeah, Mick, that's Jack. He was told to be reading *The Morning Post.*"

'No better rag to put off a Castle spotter.'

'Frank will be meeting him any second now and then they will go inside Mitchell's for lunch. A picture of innocence, isn't he, Mick?'

'As innocent and as saintly as you are, Liam! Anyway, I've seen what he looks like now, so let's be on our way for a bite to eat.'

'The Wicklow Hotel?'

'Yes, that's the closest.'

Fifteen minutes later, they sat over soup at a table close to the kitchen door.

'There's something on your mind, Mick, isn't there? About Jack.'

'Yeah. You say the ... the English fellow ... what's his name?'

Looking quickly about Liam lowered his voice further. 'Lexington. L.'

'Yeah, him. Has he been satisfied with the stuff Jack's sending him?'

'I think so, Mick. He hasn't questioned Jack on anything so far.'

'And you believe Jack when he said that's his name?'

'Absolutely! Frank has quizzed Jack closely on this. He is certain that's his name and I'm inclined to believe him.'

'Why?'

'That was the name L. gave Jack when they first met at the field hospital or whatever they called it.'

'That's according to Jack. And that was three or four years ago. Are you sure we can trust him?'

'Both of us, Frank and myself, believe we can trust Jack implicitly.'

'Why?'

'First, he didn't offer his services to us. Remember, a trusted and proven Brigade Intelligence Officer, a Brother, had him

149

well watched before recruiting him.'

'But that was just for the job in Birr, wasn't it?'

'Yeah, but Jack delivered on what was asked of him there. And since arriving in Dublin he has carried out to the letter all instructions given him. He was a reliable fallback on the tram for the Bell job, and he helped out on the Wexford shooting job. But more to the point, Mick, he's had ample opportunity to double cross us so far and he hasn't.'

'O.K., Liam.' Collins scraped his bowl. 'You have a point.'

'So, Mick – getting back to L and his name – what's bothering you about it? Why would he give a false name to Jack in the first place?'

'L's name isn't on the Army List,' Collins said flatly.

'But, Mick, giving a false name to the man who probably saved his life doesn't make sense. And as L was a serving officer at the Front in the thick of it, he was hardly in Intelligence then, was he?'

'O.K. But we still need to know his real name.'

'Does his real name matter, Mick? We have an address for him in London – through Jack, remember? – The India Club. So if we need to find him Sam Maguire could look after that.'

'Stick to Sam's codename – Tramp. According to him, that's just an accommodation address and the place where he sends his information is a butcher's shop.' Collins sat back. 'We're having it watched, but if we knew his real name – and I still bet it isn't L – we'd have a better chance of finding out more about him.'

150

'Is it that important, Mick? After all, we're not passing on state secrets.'

'As far as the other side is concerned, Liam, what they are getting are our state secrets!' He paused. 'Anyway, as far as I'm concerned, L is his cover name. It would be madness for anybody in this business to use their true names. Let's face it, the best spy the British ever had made fools of the top American Fenians for almost 20 years with that phoney French name of his...Henri le Car ... Carré ... .was it?'

'le Caron, Mick.'

'Yeah, him. I'm not going to be made a fool for a second time.'

'Like that business with the Jameson fellow?'

Collins's lips tightened. 'Who else?'

'He paid the price though, didn't he, Mick?'

'That's not the point, Liam. You must never let the enemy know you're vulnerable in any way. Especially allowing yourself fall for one of their agents.'

They fell silent as the waiter arrived to take their orders. As he walked away, Liam continued. 'I've just had a thought, Mick. L might have a temporary commission?'

'They were officially abolished at the beginning of July. If there's a list of them it's probably in a War Office cabinet somewhere.'

'So he's not on any British Army List we can check?'

'No. But he's on our List, Liam. And that's what matters.'

Liam straightened as a thought struck him. 'Is it possible we're overlooking the obvious? The address he gave Jack was the India Club. Could he be an Indian Army man?'

'I hadn't thought of that. Yes, he could well be. There has to be an Indian Army officers' list somewhere. I'll ask Tramp to check that.'

'Then I'll add that to the list of things you'll be discussing with him tomorrow in Dun Laoghaire?'

Collins smiled thinly. 'Kingstown, Liam, when we're not among our own.' He paused. 'Yes, add Mr. L's name to the list. It'll be a long meeting at the rate those lists are growing these days.'

'Just as well Tramp has the time between sailings.'

'One more thing, Mick, about L,' Liam said. 'Whatever he did during the war, we've still no idea whether he is now British Army, M.I.5, Thomson's Special Branch or Secret Service?'

'No, we don't. However, though I'm not a betting man, I'll wager L is B.A.'

'Why?'

'Because Jack is B. A. and they came together on the frontline.'

'Does it matter who he works for as long as the stuff we're feeding them is believed and acted on?'

Collins's lips tightened. 'It does matter, we need to be sure we feed the right stuff to the right source to get the right result.'

The waiter arrived with the main course.

'That Shepherd's Pie smells very appetising, Bob,' Collins said genially.

'Yes, Mr. Field. That's why I recommended it. It's got lots a beef in it,' the waiter responded.

'And how are you keeping?'

'Busy here now, thank goodness.'

'Glad to hear that.'

When he had gone, both men ate in silence for some minutes.

'A good man that, Liam. Very observant.'

'The waiter?'

'Yes. Based on his information I've made a decision to have the porter fellow ... removed for good. He's definitely on the Castle's payroll. Otherwise we'd have to give this place a wide berth.'

'Who do you want to do the job?'

'I was thinking of Jack?'

'Good choice. Nobody in Dublin knows him.'

'I meant to ask you, how is that business in London going?' Liam enquired.

'The handover of the medallions is taking place today,' Collins responded.

ooooo0000ooooo

'Miss Dempsey,' the thickset man greeted her expressionlessly. 'I believe you have a letter for me?'

'I do indeed,' Kate replied. She handed him a sealed envelope. He looked carefully at the seal, then opened the envelope and read the contents.

'Welcome to the Onion Lane Foundry, Miss Dempsey,' he said, offering a hand the size of a ham. 'You will understand my caution, I know.'

'Thank you, Mr Parker,' Kate said, trying not to wince at the iron grip. She sat on the proffered chair, resisting the impulse to wipe the seat with her handkerchief. The room was clearly the office of a senior member of the company but its leather seats and mahogany desk had undergone rough treatment over the years.

'I understand from Mr Kennedy, my principal, that there is a possibility that there may be some difficulty with the authorities?' she asked.

Parker regarded her. 'What exactly did he tell you, Miss Dempsey?'

'That the matter required strict secrecy and that it involved a quantity of Tsarist gold medallions that were struck at your foundry at about the time the War broke out?' She looked enquiringly at him. He nodded.

'They were intended to be the Tsar's personal award for all in the Imperial Russian service,' she continued, 'but most particularly to honour the officers of the Imperial Army and Navy. They were to have been collected by the Tsar's personal representative here in London, but this never occurred. They

154

are now for sale. And should the British authorities learn of their existence, there is a strong likelihood that they would be seized. Is that the case?'

'That is the situation in bare outline. Let me give you the full facts.' He picked up a pipe from the ashtray on his desk, and applied a match to the bowl. In between puffs, he continued: 'I entered a lawful commercial contract, Miss Dempsey, some months before the War broke out. I had remedies in English law for any default on the part of the other party as regards payment. But what happens?' he blew a cloud of smoke in Kate's direction. 'I'll tell you what happens. The government introduces a regulation that makes it unlawful for me to complete the contract. Why? Because the Crown says it now has control and right of possession of an essential raw material, namely gold, that I, in good faith, have legitimately obtained and paid for in order to fulfil that contract.'

'You mean, the Tsar supplied you with the gold for the medallions?' Kate asked, stifling a cough.

'In a manner of speaking, he did, yes. It was freighted from Russia as ingots, only painted grey so that they matched the rest of the cargo which was down as lead in the ship's manifest. When they arrived in London, they were off-loaded and warehoused the same week that the Archduke Ferdinand was assassinated in Sarajevo. A fellow called Prince Youssopov was to contact me, and he arrived a few days later and demanded full and immediate payment for the ingots before releasing them to me. I had to act quickly on this, you see, the banks had begun restricting credit on commercial contracts with Russia. I managed to get together 80% of the cash – and that wasn't easy, I can tell you - and he accepted that as full and final payment for the ingots. They were then delivered to my

155

foundry.'

'You have a receipt for the ingots?' Kate asked.

'I certainly do. It's secure in my safe,' he declared.

'Well, that's very good to hear, Mr Parker,' she said. 'As the ingots are the 'raw materials' for the manufacture of the medallions, they are part of your business assets. So, under English law, they remain your property until full and final payment of all sums due for the medallions. Included in that 'all sums due' are the costs and expenses arising from their secure storage since 1914.' Kate paused to allow this to sink in. 'It's not much different from an unpaid pawnbroker's right to possession of the pawned item until all monies due are paid.'

Parker stared fixedly at her, the smoke from his pipe rising into the air. 'I only paid half the value of the medallions,' he said cautiously.

'You purchased gold ingots, the raw material for the medallions,' Kate said crisply. 'You manufactured them, and they are your lawful property until fully paid for. And that means you enjoy full legal title until then. So neither the Tsar's successors nor the Bolshevist State dictatorship in Moscow have any claim whatsoever in English law on the medals you hold.'

'You certain of that, Miss Dempsey?'

'Absolutely,' she declared. She had no doubt an assiduous KC for the Crown would demolish her argument point by point, but that was neither here nor there. 'I am certain enough to conclude the contract now on behalf of my principals. I shall, however, require the receipt given you by Mr Koussopov for

156

the gold.'

Mr Parker beamed. 'I have the receipt here, together with a photograph of it taken with a box camera. You may have the photograph until full payment is made by your principals.'

'That is not acceptable. When we conclude this contract, the title and all risks pass to my principals through their agents, Messrs Fitch, O'Leary and Sedakar, attorneys in New York. That receipt will be vital in confirming my principals' paramount title to the medallions in an American court.'

Parker eyed her suspiciously. 'I don't quite understand. What is the point you are making, Miss Dempsey?'

'If the Crown were later to take issue with you as regards the medals, they will no longer be within its jurisdiction. The Crown would, however, be free to commence a legal action in the State of New York to secure them by asserting its proprietary right of possession under English law. That receipt will be vital to my principals in disproving that right. So if you insist on retaining it, there is no point in discussing this any further.' Kate gathered her gloves and handbag together and made to rise.

'Hold on just a minute please, Miss,' Mr Parker said hastily. 'You do have the $5,000 deposit with you, Miss Dempsey?'

'I do,' Kate said, taking an envelope out of her bag and handing it to him. 'It is in the form of a bill of exchange as is normal for transactions of ... of transactions like this.'

Parker examined it. 'It's drawn up by the Malayan Tea Company Limited in favour of and endorsed by a Mr Robert Briscoe. He looked up. 'I know of the Tea Company but who is this Briscoe fellow?'

'He is a respected, established and successful commercial agent in Dublin,' Kate replied with asperity. 'As you well know, all you have to do is endorse the bill then discount it with your own bank. Your account will be credited with the $5,000 less the bank's small discount fee. Or you may wish to hold the bill until it becomes due and present it for payment then?'

'I think I'd like to present this to my bank for discounting before I release the medallions,' Parker said.

'Of course, Mr Parker,' Kate said. 'That is perfectly understandable. Might I suggest you do that in the morning, or this afternoon, if you have time. We will arrange to have the medallions collected tomorrow afternoon.'

'And the balance due of $45,000?'

'As the contract states, when the medallions are delivered to Messrs Fitch, O'Leary and Sedakar in New York they, as agents of my principals, will credit the balance to a trust account already set up in a New York bank in your name. I have the details of this account ready to deliver to you when you have endorsed the bill.'

'You're asking me to place a lot of trust in your ... anonymous principals, Miss Dempsey.'

'Likewise, my principals are entering into quite a risky contract with you, Mr Parker. Messrs Fitch and Associates is both a legal entity and trustee against whom legal proceedings can be taken in the United States. But Messrs Fitch and Associates, for their part, cannot sue your firm in the United Kingdom. And, after all, until the medallions are safely in New York, they

158

might possibly go down to the bottom of the Atlantic in a storm. Or be stolen. Or confiscated by the British Government.' Kate smiled placidly at Parker. 'Mind you, once they have title to the 'goods', I'm sure they will have them insured for all contingencies.'

Parker brooded. Then he slapped the top of the desk with a sound like gunshot. 'I should like to have sight of that New York trust account, Miss Dempsey, before I endorse the bill.'

'You may certainly have sight of it in this envelope, Mr Parker.' She extracted the letter and passed it to him. He read it and returned it. 'Is that to your satisfaction?' she asked.

He nodded.

'Well, perhaps you will be good enough to call in one of your clerks to witness this transaction.' As he rose and crossed to the door, Kate breathed out in relief.

'Mr Parker,' she said. 'I have to admit that I am curious. What do the medallions look like? May I see one?'

Reaching into a desk drawer, he passed a coin over to her. Kate took it on her palm. It was about the size and thickness of a shilling piece, but heavier. 'It is, well, it's rather a small coin, isn't it?'

'It was made to the exact specifications given to me,' he said heavily. 'It has the profile of Tsar Nicholas III with his initials and below that is the date, 1914. It is not, in fact a coin. It doesn't have the milled edge that distinguishes a coin from a medallion. Had such milling been requested, I should have been obliged for legal reasons to refuse the contract.'

Kate smiled to herself at this pious expression of conscience. Almost everything to do with these medallions was illegal.

ooooo0000Oooooo

Waite fell into step beside Jack as he strolled beside the lake in Herbert Park. 'What's all this about, Jack? We're only supposed to meet like this in an emergency. You are still sending information to London, aren't you?'

'Oh yes, Mr Lexington. Are they any good to you?'

'They're excellent so far – please do keep them coming.'

'Right,' Jack said. 'They're the best I can do without sticking my neck out. Sorry about contacting you like this, Mr. Lexington, but it is a kind of an emergency. I'll have to be away from Dublin for a while the week after next and I thought you'd want to know.'

'Whatever for?' Waite asked, alarmed. 'Is something wrong? You haven't been sacked, have you?'

'Nothing's wrong. There are two reasons I wanted to talk to you. That was the first, but I've been thinking that I might be in danger and ...'

'Danger?' Waite exclaimed. 'What do you mean – danger?'

'Well, these Shinner Volunteers have been shooting people and pinning notices on their chests saying Spies Beware. They'd shoot me if they found out I'm passing information on

160

to you or whoever is getting it in London. And to tell you the truth, I think some of the fellas who are telling me things would spill the beans to the Volunteers if they put a gun to their head. If I was lucky, I might get a warning to run, but where would I go?' Jack looked as woebegone as he could.

Waite felt entirely in control. This was something he had discussed with Cromie. 'What you would do is go straight to Amiens Street Station and get the next G.N.R. train to Belfast,' he said.

'Belfast?' Jack exclaimed. 'I don't know anybody in Belfast.'

'You would book into the Railway Hotel, tell the desk clerk to telephone a number which I will give you, and say you've arrived. In no time, someone would come to pick you up.' He took out his pocket book and, tearing a page out, wrote the number down. 'Does that make you feel better?

'Thanks, Mr Lexington. That's a load off my mind,' Jack folded the paper and put it in his pocket.

'What was the other thing you wished to talk about?' Waite enquired.

'I won't be able to see you for four or five weeks,' Jack said.

'But we rarely need to meet, Jack, unless by arrangement. The Post Office Box system works perfectly.'

'Ah, but you see, I won't be here to post anything. Mr. Wright is sending me around the country to all the big racecourses. I have to meet bookies to give them his special telephone number.'

'What do you mean special?' Waite was intrigued.

'It's for what's called 'spreading bets'. Jack explained. 'That's the bookies' way of sharing a big bet with other bookies so they share the loss or the profit.'

'Are you telling me, Jack, that bookies have some way of sharing a bet on the day of a race with another bookie some miles distant?'

'Yes, Mr. Lexington, but only if they have the time to share it by telephone. Or by a 'bookie's runner,' if they have one, or even by post. Some very large bets come in the post days before some races when the odds are low. Then they have the time to share them by post.'

'Betting through the Post Office! I've never heard of such a thing.'

'You'd be surprised, Sir. Quite a few respectable people bet privately by post days before a race, people who would not be seen dead near a bookie's shop. But if a lot of the money is being wagered on the day, the bookie will only take some bets if he has the time to share them by telephone or by using a 'runner' to other bookies.'

'Well, it all seems very complicated to me, Jack. When I was at Bellewstown races, there was no telephone apparatus. So what would a bookie do there?

So Mr Lexington had been at Bellewstown and they hadn't seen each other. Well, thank God for that, Jack thought. But was he a pal of Eddie's? Or Mr Tweed?

'Well, the bookie could refuse to take the bet, but if he took it, he'd tick-tack the other bookies to lay it off.' Seeing Waite's look of mystification, Jack added helpfully 'That's the sign language the bookies use to talk to each other about odds and things.'

Waite frowned. 'As regards your being away, does that mean your ex-servicemen will have to hold on to any information they've got?'

'Yes, Sir, I'm sorry about that. But you never know what might be waiting for me when I get back.'

'One last thing, Jack,' Waite said. 'When you mentioned the Shinners might ... get you unawares, well, I did the best thing I could for you by getting you that Belfast number. It also occurred to me that, if anything should happen to you ...'

Jack was offended. 'Like what, Mr Lexington?'

'Well, you could be knocked down by a motor car crossing the road – so I thought it might be a good idea for me to meet one or two of your better informants. What do you think?'

Jack assumed a thoughtful expression. 'That would be a great idea, Mr Lexington,' he said gravely. 'I'll have to talk to them, though.' Let Mr Staunton look after this one, he thought.

As they parted, Jack whistled as he walked away. What would Mr. Lexington say if he knew that, instead of visiting bookies he, Jack, was taking a trip to London to pick up a Rolls Royce with a special cargo. He was to drive it to Liverpool and then it would be loaded onto a cargo steamer bound for Dublin.

ooooo0000ooooo

Liam Tobin clattered into the bedroom of the house in Clonliffe Road. Michael Collins sat at a table, absorbed in documents.

'You were right, Mick, Lexington wasn't that fella's real name after all.'

Collins looked up. 'Yes,' he said. 'I know. I asked Tramp to organise someone to check out his India Club membership. His man greased the palm of one of the servants there, and got Waite's Army number.' Opening a notebook, he flicked through a few pages. 'Ah, yes, here we are ... it's No.07/27055 – for what that's worth, now that we know his real name and his home address.'

'Where is the India Club?' Staunton enquired.

'Aldwych.'

'We must have been close to the India Club when we were in that Aldwych restaurant with Tramp the last time we were in London,' Staunton asked, settling himself on the bed's bare springs.

'That's irrelevant,' Collins grunted.

'Still a coincidence, Mick. Anyway, are you going to show this to Frank?'

'No. Not for now. But I'll pass the information on to Dick.'

'Why would you tell Mulcahy!' Staunton was nonplussed. 'Isn't he up to his neck in Volunteer Organisation and Operations stuff?'

'No, Dick McKee. O.C. Dublin Brigade.'

'But hasn't he got enough on his plate organising Units for the ... the List?'

'He has.' Collins gathered up his papers.

Tobin grinned. 'Ah, I think I see what you're getting at! You're not going to add Waite's name to the List now, are you, Mick?'

'Yes, Liam, I am.'

Chapter 7

'...Lloyd George had an amazing theory that Tudor or someone was murdering two Sinn Féiners to every loyalist the S.F.'s murdered...'

Sir Henry Wilson, Diaries, 12th July 192

Liam looked up as Frank Staunton entered. 'I've got news, Frank. Interesting news about Mr so-called Lexington.'

'So-called?'

'His real name is Captain L.S. Waite, Indian Army,' Liam said tersely.

'That explains why he was not on the British Army List?'

'Exactly! So, on balance, it's safe to say that he is in Military Intelligence of some sort. But we still don't know whether he has any connection with the British Army's own Dublin District Special Branch or with that new shifty group here with connections to the Special Branch at Scotland Yard in London. The one thing we are pretty sure of is that Waite has nothing to do with the R.I.C.'s own Intelligence section. So knowing that he has connections with Military Intelligence is enough to have him shot. His name has been added to the list of British spies in Dublin to be plugged.

'But, Liam, how ...?'

'Bear with me, Frank. Adding him to the Sunday list creates a difficulty that we knew would arise sooner or later. But we had to wait until McKee had drawn up rosters of Volunteers from the Dublin Brigade who were the right stuff for this job.'

'What do you mean, the right stuff, Liam? They all know how to shoot, don't they?'

'Of course. They have had enough training so they have no problem shooting the enemy – at a distance! But all of the Company O.C.'s reported that quite a few Volunteers couldn't face shooting an unarmed man face-to-face or in the back, enemy or not. So we can't risk having one of our lads getting a fit of conscience or cold feet at the last minute. He'd be a risk to the rest of his unit if the 'target' took the initiative and made a grab for his gun.' He paused. 'The fact is, Frank, only a handful of Volunteers in each of these special units can be relied upon to do the actual shooting. The others will be on guard or lookout duty. But they will all do their damnedest if their unit actually comes under attack.'

'Is Jack one of the reliable ones?'

'You bet he is. In fact McKee – and you won't believe this – McKee has picked him to be one of the key shooters to plug Waite.'

'But why would we want to have him shot? Isn't he more useful to us alive than dead?'

'We don't want him dead. But we could only deal with that problem when we received McKee's list of units and their targets' names and addresses. And that only arrived yesterday.'

'Ah! So I take it McKee doesn't know anything about Jack's connection with Waite/Lexington?'

'He knows absolutely nothing. He may be Commandant of the Dublin Brigade, but he doesn't need to know all the details of our Intelligence activities.'

Liam laughed. 'No more than I do when you take account of Mick Collin's hugger-mugger and mystery contacts everywhere!'

'Does Jack know his unit is targeting Waite?'

'No, not yet, but he will be told tomorrow when his Company O.C. tells him and the other Volunteers in his squad. All of the

168

shooting squads will meet separately in the late afternoon for their final instructions. So you can get in touch with Jack as early as possible tomorrow – he'll be at work almost all day.'

'I'll call at his lodgings in the morning before he leaves for work.'

'Good idea, Frank. Yes, do that.'

'What exactly am I to say?'

'Order him to make contact with Waite reasonably close to curfew and warn him that on no account is he to go near or stay in his lodgings tomorrow night.'

'Can we not get the decision to plug Lexington countermanded?'

'We could but we won't, I just told you why,' Liam went on impatiently. 'We still need Waite to be around and we need him to tell his boss that Jack saved his life. That will make the information Jack is passing on even more believable.'

'But ...'

'No buts, Frank. I've discussed all of this with Mick. Both he and Dick Mulcahy agree there is no other way to handle this if we are to continue our own ... operations successfully. Waite will have plenty of time to bolt.'

'But how will Jack make contact with Waite from then on?'

'He won't, but he'll continue to send information to the India Club. And if and when Waite or his boss decide to get in touch with Jack, they have his address. So, as I've said, with Jack saving Waite's life, his credibility is copper fastened and we can rely on Waite's boss to make direct contact soon enough with Jack. And it's business as usual from then on.'

Pointing his finger at Staunton, he continued. 'I needn't tell you this is all most secret information.'

'I've forgotten everything you've said, Liam. I promise!'

ooooo0000ooooo

Cromie was ebullient. 'You'll be pleased to hear, Waite, that a few nights ago we almost nabbed Mulcahy in his bed – I repeat, in his bed! He had the luck of the devil – minutes before our raid on his den he escaped in his pyjamas. We found his street clothes draped over a chair beside his bed. It was still warm!"

'Wasn't he seen by anybody in the street?'

'No, he got away across the rooftops!' Cromie laughed. 'Can you imagine our G.O.C. here attempting that from his Royal Hospital billet?'

'General Macready? Well, not quite, Sir, as after all the rebels are hardly ready for that yet.'

'And never will be, Waite, if we do our job. However, the good news is that, even though Mulcahy slipped through our fingers, he left behind – in addition to his clothes –a treasure trove of Volunteer H.Q. papers. We found the plans for blowing up the Liverpool docks and warehouses as well as targets in Manchester.'

'But didn't the Shinners carry out that bombing a few days ago?'

'Yes indeed,' Cromie said. 'The bombs had gone off, but these papers link him directly to that atrocity.'

'Then that raid on Mulcahy's room was most timely.'

'Oh, yes. And it was all thanks, well, in part to Jack's information.'

'Only in part?' Waite enquired.

'Yes. You see, Jack's separate information to Waite a few hours later confirmed the plans originated in Mulcahy's den which is, by the way, rather surprisingly in a quite respectable southside Dublin suburb. But in addition to the bombing plans, we also found evidence of a plot to infect officers and men with typhoid germs in contaminated milk being delivered to various barracks.'

'Good Lord!' Waite exclaimed.

'And that's not all!' Cromie went on grimly. 'We also seized their plans to spread glanders among horses of the mounted regiments.'

'What are glanders, Sir?'

'It is a very dangerous and contagious disease of horses. Quite revolting.' Cromie's mouth twisted in disgust. 'The poor brutes develop quantities of pus in their nostrils and the glands of the lower jaw set like cement. Appalling.'

'But how on earth would they infect horses with such a disease?'

171

'By contaminating their oat feed sacks somewhere *en route* in deliveries to barracks. Simply piercing the sacks with a bayonet or a knife smeared with the glanders bacillus would be enough.'

'That is dreadful!'

'Yes, Waite, especially when you consider how these Irish trumpet their love of horses. Anyway, none of us imagined that the Shinners would go even further than the Huns. They were the first to introduce chemical warfare but now the Shinners are the first with plans for germ warfare. So you can see the measure of the threat we are dealing with here?'

'Oh, yes, Sir, it is most serious. The germ warfare matter, I mean.'

'Nevertheless, Waite, we are winning. At last we are getting on top of the Collins-Mulcahy gang. Arrests of Volunteers and the seizures of weapons are all increasing. And now we have Dublin saturated with men like yourself, beavering away and finding the key terrorists.'

Waite was immediately alert. This was Cromie's first revelation that he, Waite, also had numerous 'colleagues' in Ireland? Why hadn't he mentioned them before? After all, they faced a common enemy.

'Unlike you, many of them work by night and sleep by day,' Cromie went on.

Waite thought fast. 'Do they go out with the police patrols?'

'Some do, but the Auxiliary officers and the other constables do the actual raids, while the hush-hush men watch on from the darkness. I'm glad to say our detection methods are getting better every day. For instance, plans are afoot to photograph every Sinn Féin gunman we arrest and build up a photographic reference library of terrorists. Then they can be copied anytime and distributed as required. And work is being done at a very senior level in the use of hidden microphones to see if we can eavesdrop on prisoners in cells.'

'And I suppose, Sir, as the curfew is now being enforced in Dublin with the Auxiliary patrols, the Shinners no longer have the run of the streets at night time?'

'Yes, Waite, that was the plan. And it is working. And also, thanks to the transformation of the RIC by the Auxiliary Division, law and order is gradually being restored throughout the countryside.'

'That's good news.'

'The second piece of good news I have for you, I'm delighted to say – though I am not really supposed to tell you – is that Jack seems to have tapped into the mother lode!'

'Really! In what way, may I ask?' Waite was chagrined not to be entitled to claim this good news.

'I cannot go into the details but we've been able to get our hands on a chunk of the Mulcahy/Collins war chest. In fact so far, well in excess of £15,000 in cash with, I'm told, more to come. When one of the addresses Jack's informant passed on was searched, they found a book hollowed out and containing signed blank cheques! One of our men went into the bank branch that issued the cheque book and cashed the first of the cheques for a four figure sum. When this was paid out without question, our man, after a decent interval, returned several times over a few weeks and diminished the trove with not a question asked. This, it seems, is exactly the type of spurious Shinner account that Bell had been attempting to uncover before he was murdered.'

'How did the man from the ... Castle know he could go in to the bank and present a cheque for a four figure sum in the first place?'

'Once you have the account name or number there are ways of finding out such things.'

'Was it an Irish bank?'

'Well, apart from telling you it was not a branch of the Sinn Féin Bank which we closed down in January last, I can't answer your question other than to say the bank in question was in the commercial centre of the city.'

'And if the ...'

Cromie raised his hand. 'No more questions, Waite. In fact, as I've said, you are not supposed to know anything about it at all. The whole affair remains secret. The Shinners won't mention it as they'd lose face. And we will certainly make no mention of it for fear of endangering Jack's informant.'

Waite couldn't understand why the Shinners' propaganda machine would not trumpet blatant bank robbery on the part of Government officials. But best to keep such thoughts to oneself.

'As regards Jack, Sir ...'

'Yes, I was coming to that. Have you managed to arrange my meeting with his contact?'

'I did bring the matter up with him, but he said he'd have to handle it very carefully.'

'And ...?'

'When I spoke with him yesterday he said his man was now willing to come forward but only under certain strict conditions.'

'Which are?'

'He'd have those conditions when a place, date and time were all agreed together.'

'You did tell him there is a guarantee there'll be no threat to his informant?'

'I did assure him of that, yes.'

'So have you any idea when the meeting will be?'

'Soon is all he could tell me.'

'Look, Waite, if it is a matter of money then we have it. Remember – again between ourselves – our funds for this work have increased by £15,000, thanks to Jack, and there is more to come. And there is no Treasury scrutiny through Cox and Company. And that means we can be even more generous in paying for the right information. Jack, too, will share nicely in that Shinner's cash hoard.'

Cromie's disclosure of the Treasury's minute interest in Government expenditure on Army and police hanky-panky in Ireland was another eye opener. And also that Cox and Company to whom he posted his own non-H.& C. expenses note was an actual firm and not just a front company.

'So, Waite, get working on having Jack's informant meet me.'

'Yes, Sir.'

ooooo0000ooooo

Clive gazed at the paper he held. Albert had written that the name of the driver in the photograph with Toplis was a Patrick O'Grady who was aged 18 years in 1918. He had joined the Royal Dublin Fusiliers in 1915. During the War in 1916, his regiment had been at a battlefront area, not far from F.X. Booth's regiment. His army records stated that he was an orphan, his next of kin being a John O'Grady (uncle), of Ballybeg, Kinnity, King's County.

Clive picked up the 'phone. 'Get me Major Anderson, please,' he said. 'Ah, thank you for this report, Albert. The logical next step would be to return the file to the Judge Advocate's office for him to decide what should be done next. He paused. 'Indeed, that is a very good idea. Yes, I quite agree that you should meet the RIC Liaison Inspector here in London and talk to him about passing on our request that an enquiry be carried out to see if O'Grady is now residing with his uncle. If he is, he is to be arrested and held pending an Army escort conveying him here. Keep me posted.'

ooooo0000ooooo

Leaving his bicycle outside the bookie's shop in Capel Street, Staunton stood back as a couple of off-duty British Army soldiers emerged. Not for the first time it struck him that this was a truly odd war. These men were enemy soldiers yet they walked about the city freely without fear of attack from the Volunteers. Sometimes, late at night in certain city districts, drink released old prejudices in street fights, but these rarely resulted in fatalities. With so many young Irishmen in the British Army on leave or recently discharged since the War's end, this wasn't surprising. The off-duty Tommy was welcomed by publicans, fish & chip shops, cinemas, music halls and, of course, bookies. And this bookie's shop was no different from the rest with its stale smoky atmosphere and bare floor littered with cigarette butts and crumpled betting receipts.

Entering, he spotted Jack who stood at the back behind the counter. Their eyes met. Staunton indicated outside with a jerk of his head. Jack stayed expressionless. Twenty minutes later, Jack emerged and headed to a teahouse near the Fruit & Vegetable market. The hectic activity of the early hours of the market had died down.

Staunton was waiting at a table furthest from the door, hunched over a mug of tea. Jack sat facing him. He came to the point. 'You've had your instructions about tomorrow's job, Jack?'

'Yes, Mr Staunton.'

'And you have a name and address?'

'No, Mr Staunton, we'll be told all that at meeting of the unit later on today.'

'Well, between ourselves, Jack, I can tell you that among the

177

men your unit will be visiting is our friend Mr. Lexington.'

Jack was lost for words. He could only shake his head in disbelief.

'Tell me, Jack, does the name Waite mean anything to you?'

Jack hid his confusion by frowning as if he were thinking hard. And then it all came back to him. Yes, Waite was Mr. Lexington's real name. He knew all along Lexington wasn't right, but for the life of him until now he could never remember what his defender had been called in that French courtroom. So Waite had been holding out on him from the beginning!

'I've racked my brains, Mr Staunton, but the name Waite doesn't mean anything to me,' he said. Staunton hadn't given a hint that he had any suspicions about himself. Well, that was a relief. So how to play this? Percy always said – brazen it out. More often than not, it worked.

'He was telling me lies, then, Mr Staunton, wasn't he?' Jack said bleakly.

'What did you expect from a spy, Jack?'

Staunton should talk! They knew full well Waite was a spy before they found out his real name, so what did they expect of him but to do his job as a spy!

'What will I do now, Mr Staunton?'

'Tomorrow evening your unit will be given Waite's name and the address in Ely Place Upper – that's close to Stephen's Green. On the dot of 9 a.m. on Sunday morning your squad will enter his lodgings and you in particular will be one of the three picked to do the actual shooting.'

A curl of anger stirred inside Jack. He had been passing on information to Waite for them and now suddenly they want to shoot him. What the fuck was going on? What had Waite done?

Staunton continued. 'Tell me, Jack, how would you feel about shooting Waite?'

'Why should I shoot him?' Jack said truculently.

'Would you?' Staunton persisted.

'I wouldn't like it, ' Jack said reluctantly. 'But if I'm ordered to do it ...'

'Why wouldn't you like it?' Staunton asked.

'He never done me no harm, Mr Staunton. That's why.'

Staunton sat back. 'That's a good reason. If I were you, I think I'd feel the same way.'

Jack observed him warily. What the hell was going on! Why was Staunton now all matey-matey about Waite?

'Why are you asking me these questions, Mr Staunton?'

'Because when your squad leader gives you the name and address of Waite as the man your unit is to target, you will say nothing and keep a straight face. You'll all be issued with arms and instructed to leave your homes or lodgings at eight o'clock on Sunday morning and to make your way to Waite's lodgings in Ely Place. All of you are to be together there at the front door at five minutes to nine. No sooner and no later. When the job is done, all unit members will disperse with each man leaving in different directions and all with a different place to dump your guns safely.' Staunton paused. 'You'll be warned not to drink and to stay indoors until morning in case of trouble, also to be sure of a good night's sleep so that you're on your toes in the morning. Do you understand all that?'

'Yes, Mr. Staunton, Sir, I do.' Jack said sullenly. Did Staunton think he was a gom?

'Good! Because I am now giving you a countermanding order, Jack. So listen carefully to what I say.' Having given Jack his instructions, he repeated them.

'Then what do I do, Mr. Staunton?'

'Then you leave immediately and return to your lodgings. Do you understand?'

'Yes, Sir.' Jack thought fast. 'But if it's too late for me to get back to my lodgings in time before curfew, what do I do then? '

'Can you ride a bike - do you have one?'

'Yes, Mr. Staunton, I do but I might still not be able to get back to my lodgings until it's too close to curfew.'

Staunton deliberated. 'Alright, if that's the situation tonight, stay in Finn's Hotel at the end of Nassau Street - they'll keep the bike safe in the back. Call by there this evening and book yourself in. Pay them in advance.'

'Will they have a room to spare?' Jack enquired, 'with all the people coming up from the country for the match in Croke Park tomorrow?'

'Tell them Mr. Field sent you.'

'Who's Mr. Field?'

Staunton gave him a cold stare. 'They'll know.'

'One other thing, Mr Staunton, when I talk to Mr.Lex ... I mean Waite ...will I call him Mr. Waite?'

Staunton rose and buttoned his jacket. 'Yeah, do that, Jack.' He smiled. 'That'll wake him up.'

ooooo0000ooooo

After a brief knock, the door of Clive's office swung open, revealing Albert with a tray in his arms. 'I'm your maidservant for the day, Clive,' he smiled. 'I encountered your man in the corridor.'

He laid the tray on Clive's desk. 'Shall I be mother?'

Clive grunted. 'Have you news of that O'Grady?' He reached for his cup.

'Regrettably, no,' Albert said, settling down with his coffee. 'According to the RIC, he wasn't at that address, no one knows of any man of that name ever having lived there, and there is no 'uncle'. In fact, there is no such place as the 'Parish of Ballybeg' anywhere in King's County and there is no O'Grady in what they call the Townland of Kinnity. Most annoying.'

'So John O'Grady was a false name from the beginning,' Clive said.

'Indeed. However, there is one curious thing – when I mentioned to the RIC Inspector that O'Grady had been a wartime deserter, he laughed. It seems he had received a request a few months ago from the Army in King's County regarding another deserter from the Army barracks there. As if, the Inspector said, they hadn't enough on their plates already with the mayhem caused by the Shinners. Anyway, this deserter fellow's name was John O'Reilly and, what is more interesting, a photograph of this deserter is available.'

'What we need from them is a photograph of our man, O'Grady, Albert. The O'Reilly fellow is a matter for Irish Command, for the attention of General Macready, the G.O.C. there. It's no business of ours.'

'So we can forget this O'Reilly fellow?' Albert asked.

'I think so. It's far too convenient a coincidence for this to be our man. In fact, I rather think that this is an end of this matter.'

Albert swung a polished shoe. 'Very well, if you say so, Clive. It's been a most interesting enquiry, not merely in itself but also in the tit-bits which surfaced during it.' He cocked a satirical eye at Clive, who did not react. 'Such as the fact that Sir Henry twice failed his Military Academy Entrance Examination,' he added.

Clive was impassive. 'I am aware of that, Albert.'

Albert was crestfallen. 'Then how on earth did he receive his commission?'

Clive smiled. 'He did what any young gentleman of more ambition than scholarship did in those days: he purchased a commission in the local Longford Militia, and after a decent interval transferred across to the Army.'

Albert beamed. 'Well, well, well!' he said. 'A lot of duffers took that route.'

'And did you know that Johnny French was one of them?'

Albert's jaw dropped. 'Our Lord Lieutenant and Governor General of Ireland? What militia did he join?'

'None.' Clive drained his cup. 'He joined the Navy as an ordinary seaman in Portsmouth. After a decent interval, he transferred to the Army.'

'So Johnny French was once a matelot. Fancy that.'

Clive stood. 'Where shall we dine, Cavalry or Blades? And you know nothing of French's early years.' He shot Albert a severe look.

'Cavalry. Blades is swamped these days with field commission johnnies. And I have absolutely no idea of what you speak, Clive.' Albert responded.

ooooo0000ooooo

Kate and Waite emerged arm in arm from the restaurant onto a bitterly cold Nassau Street. Kate drew the collar of her coat up around her neck.

'That was such a lovely evening, Stephen,' she smiled up at him. 'The performance in the Gaiety was wonderful, and that was an excellent dinner.'

'Jammet's certainly lived up to its reputation,' Waite said. 'It is a shame the evening has to end, but curfew is only an hour away. Time for you to leave for home, yes?'

'Not home,' Kate said. 'Remember? I've been spending nights in my great-aunt's house in Glasnevin until her live-in housekeeper returns. It looks as though I will be there for some time yet. Nora's mother is far more seriously ill than she thought. A very good neighbour keeps an eye on Aunt when her daily maid leaves at six, but it is at night that we feel someone must be there just in case my Aunt is taken ill.'

'Let's stroll up to the Shelbourne Hotel,' Waite suggested. 'There's bound to be a cab there. And in the meantime, we can discuss what we will do tomorrow.'

As they walked, Kate slipped her arm through his. 'Why don't we meet in the Green at 11.30 – weather permitting?' she said.

'Good idea,' Waite said. 'We can watch the children feeding the ducks in the pond and then we'll have lunch – where would you like to eat?'

'Perhaps the Bonne Bouche,' Kate suggested.

'Then the Bonne Bouche it is, my lady,' Waite did a mock bow.

Kate sobered. 'It's just occurred to me, Stephen, that perhaps we had better eat quite early. There's a major football match in Croke Park playing field tomorrow and there will be lots of people in town.'

'Ah,' Waite agreed. 'Then let's aim to eat at 12.30.'

184

As their cab clopped its way through the city centre, they looked out at the busy pavements where Dubliners were making their way home. Waite took her hand in his.

'Aren't you being rather forward, Mr Lexington?' Kate said in mock indignation. 'I trust you are not sitting on my evening bag.'

Waite made a play of rummaging about on the seat and held it up. 'Habeo!' he said.

'You are unable to remember the Latin name for a handbag, Mr Lexington? I am shocked.'

'I regret I cannot, Miss Swanton. But perhaps you do?' He embraced her awkwardly. Unresisting, she allowed him to kiss her lightly. He pressed on with a full, deep and sustained kiss until the discomfort of their embrace drew him back, breathless.

'Kate,' he murmured. 'We've known each other for several months now. But we've never been alone together, like this. As close and ...'

'Intimate?' she breathed.

'Exactly,' he said, taking her into his arms once more. In the dimness, he regarded her lovely face, eyes closed and lips parted. Suffused with passion, and drawing her even closer, she responded to his intense kiss. A few seconds later, she pushed him gently away, while taking a deep breath.

'Stephen, you are a naughty boy, taking advantage of a maiden in a carriage!'

Immediately contrite, Waite blurted out the first thing that came to mind. 'I do apologise, Kate. I have been too forward.'

She smiled at him. 'In the nicest possible way, Stephen. We're approaching Doyle's Corner, which means we are only a few minutes from Lindsay Road. Draw the curtain on your side ...'

All too soon, the jarvey tapped on the cab roof. 'Lindsay Road in a minute or two, Sir.'

In the darkened porch of her great-aunt's house, they shared a last clinging embrace.

'I must go in now before a neighbour spots us.'

'They would really require remarkable eyesight to see us in the darkness,' Waite smiled. 'Tomorrow morning, then, in Stephen's Green?'

He swung back to the waiting cab. 'To Ely Place, please, driver,' he said, hardly hearing his response.

When the cab reached Sackville Street the driver stopped. 'Sorry, Sir, this is as far as I go. It's nearly curfew.' Waite looked at his watch. Fifteen minutes to curfew. Paying the man, he strode towards Ely Place, cutting along Nassau Street and then up Merrion Square.

As he walked, he rebuked himself for not taking an opportunity to clear the decks between himself and Kate and to end once and for all his continuing deceit in failing to tell her the truth about his real purpose in Ireland. Each time they met, he resolved to tell her, but each time, delighting in her company, he postponed disclosing his double life. How could they have a future together in mutual love, trust and confidence if he were to shut her off from an intrinsic element of his life?

It went against the grain to keep secrets from her, but his work here was a duty, the patriotic duty of all Englishman. It sprang naturally from one's inner self. For Waite, it was an impulse he believed was natural to all Englishmen - an abiding love of his mother country, the centre of the world's most civilized, diverse and far flung Empire. England was not an imperial state in the sense of the former Kaiser's Germany. It was a benign constitutional monarchy under the very constitutional King George V. As a citizen and yet a soldier and officer - in a manner of speaking - he regarded that his duty was owed to his king and to England's democratic system. Although India was the land of his birth, his duty still lay to England. He acknowledged that India would inevitably have Home Rule. That was the consensus in the smoking rooms of every club he had ever entered. But that would not happen for at least forty or fifty years hence. Like the Irish, they were not quite ready for it yet. Indeed, whatever constitutional posturing the Indian National Congress Party adopted, everyone knew it was undoubtedly encouraging - whether directly or indirectly - the Bengali Nationalists. Already, those extremists were creating expectations among the uneducated masses that were impossible to realize. Together with the Bengali unrest, the lurking nightmare of every English resident there was of a second Indian Mutiny. It was an unspoken fear, but no less real for that.

As to the present, when the alternatives had been outlined to him by Cromie in January, he had been ready and willing - notwithstanding an initial hesitation - to accept Ireland as his first assignment on 'special service' to his King. A chilling thought struck him. What if he were to confide in Kate, and

187

the revelation were so shocking to her as to end their relationship? Thank goodness he had said nothing. Before he shared the information with her, he must prepare for all of her possible reactions. Dash it! Even thinking like this made him feel a calculating cad.

Waite walked past the new, almost complete Royal University buildings. Ely Place ahead seemed deserted. Slowing his pace, he continued towards his digs at the end of Upper Ely Place where the *cul de sac* ended at the rear gates of St Vincent's Hospital. One of the gates was opening. It struck Waite as being a little odd at this hour. A man was emerging, probably a hospital worker on the way home before curfew, Waite reflected. The man drew nearer.

'Mr. Lexington? Shhhh!'

It was Jack.

'Don't stay in your lodgings tonight, Mr. Lexington.' Jack said in low voice.' I repeat, do not stay in your lodgings tonight. They know you are Stephen Waite and they are coming to get you.'

And then he had pushed past. Shocked initially at hearing his own name, and then by the realisation that his carefully constructed persona was now known to the Shinners, Lexington continued ahead as if in a trance as he grappled with Jack's warning. Outside his lodgings, he hesitated for a few seconds and then continued on to the Hospital gates, now firmly shut. Crossing to the other pavement, his first instinct was to get as far away from Ely Place as possible before curfew. He walked rapidly into St. Stephen's Green. Where could he go? Should he book into the Shelbourne Hotel opposite?

188

Common sense dictated that an hotel closer to the city centre would be better. But there was little time left now.

Walking down Kildare Street he tried to fathom what was behind Jack's warning? What exactly was the danger? Racking his brain he could not recall having done anything that would have attracted suspicion to himself. Had he failed to take some precaution? 'They are going to get you,' Jack had said. When? Tonight? Tomorrow? The curfew would end at 5.00 a.m. and few would be out and about before 9.00 a.m. on a Sunday. But would whatever Jack had warned him about occur during curfew? Jack's warning could not be ignored. He had to make sure that they could not find him. The best thing would be to stay in an hotel. Finn's Hotel around the corner from the bottom of Kildare Street was the nearest. But could he be sure of a vacant room in such a small hotel at this hour? Better try the Royal Hibernian Hotel in Dawson Street.

As he entered, his breathing calmed as he encountered the affable smile of the manager, M. Bresson, who recognized him as a regular visitor in both the lounge and restaurant and seemed to take it as quite natural that a late and unexpected guest required a room, although without luggage. 'It is no problem, Mr. Waite,' he assured him. 'From time to time, the curfew drives in unexpected guests who missed the last tram and were unable to find a cab. Perhaps you would be in need of shaving equipment?' He beckoned to a porter and waved Waite to the stairs.

With the hotel closed for the night, Waite felt he could think and calm his racing thoughts. He sat in his room's armchair with a double whiskey and relaxed.

The delayed shock of Jack's warning had struck home in the

past few minutes. For the first time in his life he felt truly vulnerable, alone and in real danger. An awareness at least of the perils attached to Cromie's work ought first have come home the day following his first visit to Dublin when he had read of the callous shooting dead of that old man – Mr. Bell? – in broad daylight and in full view of his fellow tram passengers and passers-by. But why had he, Waite, been picked out? For the life of him, he could not remember what he had done wrong. He had never carried a gun. He did not leave a scrap of paper in his lodgings that might indicate his secret work. Indeed, once he had taken note of Jack's lists, they and the envelope that held them had been burned to ashes in the fireplace of his room and he had raked the ashes to powder. Yet the fact was the Shinners now knew his identity.

Chapter 8

'They got what they deserved. Beaten by counterjumpers.'

Lloyd George, 23 November 1920

(as told to author by P. Moylett: *Michael Collins*, Rex Taylor (1958)

Kate sat on the easy chair beside the cooking range. The light in the kitchen was dim, lit by only one gas mantle. When coming in from the cold, she was in the habit of warming up in the kitchen before making a dash for her equally frigid bedroom. The distant rumble of her great-aunt's heavy snoring broke the silence. She smiled. It was curious how someone so ladylike and so very deaf could produce such a noise. She glanced at the clock. It was close to 12.30 a.m. Gathering up her discarded coat and gloves, she made her way in the dark along the passageway leading to the hall. She stopped short as somebody banged on the hall door. The noise reverberated through the house.

'Open up! Open up!' a man's voice bellowed.

Kate froze. What on earth ... no, it couldn't be. Auxiliaries? A raid? She thought fast. She had occasionally placed compromising documents behind the books in the sitting room, confident that her aunt would never go near them, but there was nothing incriminating in the house now. She was sure of that. Approaching the front door along the hallway, all she could see through its decorative glass panels were faint blurred images against the darkness outside. As she opened it, she was momentarily blinded as powerful torches focused on her face.

'Put your hands up, Miss! Search her, Sergeant Scrope,' a commanding voice said. She said nothing, but glared at where the voice seemed to be coming from.

'Nothing on her, Captain.'

One of the torches was lowered sufficiently for her to see that the officer was probably no older than herself.

'Who's in this house now, Miss?'

'Just my elderly aunt and myself. There's no one else here.' Kate said icily.

'And your name is?'

'Catherine Swanton.'

'We are going to search this house. From top to bottom.'

At a signal from the captain, the torches were extinguished. Straightaway, the facade and hallway of the house were flooded with intense white light from a searchlight mounted on a Black and Tan tourer parked on the roadway outside. Soldiers pushed past her where she stood, guarded by Scrope. As more armed Tan 'constables' entered, the Auxiliary officer barked instructions. 'Mackay, Harris and Keith, search the back garden and any outhouses and sheds.'

'Yes, Sir.'

'You, Eden and Wickham, the kitchen and pantry. Oliphant, take Jarvis and Cardwell and search the dining and sitting room. Oh, and don't forget under the stairs. And you three, upstairs.'

As they were about to ascend the stairs, Kate started forward, ignoring her guard.

'My great aunt is in the front bedroom above. She is very deaf. Your men will give her a dreadful shock if they go in to her room and wake her up. She may have a heart attack.'

'We have our orders, Miss,' the officer said.

'I insist on being with your men when they enter her room and on being the person to wake her up. Or you may take the consequences of terrorising an old lady, possibly to her death,' Kate said. She held his gaze. To her relief, he conceded.

'Very well, Miss. You may open the door and enter the room first. But remember, no tricks! We have you covered.'

Kate ran up the stairs and turned up the gas mantle outside her aunt's room.

As she knocked loudly on the door, the Auxiliary officer and his Tans stood to one side. Beside her great aunt's bed she spoke as loudly as she could. 'Aunt Eileen, Aunt Eileen! Wake up!'

The old lady roused and blinked at her, bewildered. 'Surely it isn't morning already, Kate?'

Kate, shouting, answered.

'No, Aunt Eileen. It is after midnight.'

'What's the matter, Kate? Is something wrong? There isn't a fire, is there?'

'No, Aunt. There is no fire. A prisoner has escaped from Mountjoy Jail and he is believed to be in the neighbourhood.'

'Get the Constabulary!'

'The Constabulary are already here, Aunt Eileen. And they wish to search the house and make sure that rogue isn't hiding anywhere.'

'Oh, thank God for that. But make sure they search the back garden and sheds as well. He could easily have come in from the railway line behind.'

Kate continued. 'Now, Aunt Eileen, I'm going to put the gas light on. So I want you to pull the bedcovers over your head while the Constables....' she paused deliberately, 'while the Constables here make sure there is nobody hiding in your bedroom. And I shall stay here while they do that.'

The three Tans tramped in. One stood at the door, pistol at the ready. Another opened the wardrobe and poked about with the barrel of his rifle, then crossed to the curtains and pulled the drapes aside. The third ransacked the chest of drawers, then lay on the floor and shone his torch under the old lady's bed. A few minutes later, their task completed, their officer ordered them to search the other bedrooms.

As quickly as she could, Kate stuffed the scattered clothing back into the drawers. Reaching up to the gas mantle she gave the chain a light tug. In complete darkness except for the glimmer, she shouted at her aunt.

'It's alright now, Aunt Eileen, you can draw back the covers now.'

There was no answer. Drawing them aside herself, Kate smiled involuntarily on hearing a gentle snore. She closed the door. Two of the Tans were waiting outside. They escorted her downstairs to the hallway and about fifteen minutes later the Auxiliary officer returned. He stared grimly at her.

'My men have completed their search of the rest of the house.'

Just then one of the Tans emerged from the sitting room.

'Anything incriminating there?'

'No, Sir.'

Kate breathed a silent sigh of relief. She had had a niggling fear that she might have left something compromising behind the books. The Auxiliary officer turned to her. Relaxing now at the prospect of the ordeal being over, she was shocked alert by his last words.

'... that you are now under arrest.'

'Excuse me, what did you say, Officer?'

'I said, Miss Swanton, I have to inform you that you are now under arrest.'

In an effort to buy time she asked a question she knew to be futile.

'May I have sight of your arrest warrant, please?'

'Under the Restoration of Order in Ireland Act, Miss Swanton, which came into effect on the 1st September last, I am not required to have such a warrant. My orders are to arrest you once these premises have been searched. So you will accompany us now. Get your coat.'

'But what about my great aunt? She will be in the house on her own.'

'You ought to have thought about that before getting involved with the Shinners.'

'I have no idea what you are talking about,' Kate answered with as much dignity as she could muster. 'I am appalled that you would punish an old lady for your misapprehensions. At least let me leave a note for her, she will be so worried if she wakes up in an empty house.'

'Outside, Miss,' he said.

A couple of minutes later, as Kate sat fuming on a bench in the back of a lorry waiting outside, the Auxiliary officer looked at his watch.

'Oh, by the way, Miss Swanton, I should tell you your employer, Mr. O'Brien, should also be under arrest by now,' he said before taking his seat in the tourer.

ooooo00000ooooo

Jack woke suddenly. It was still dark. He checked his watch. There was plenty of time to get to Ely Place before 8.55 a.m. He washed and shaved using the cold water in the washstand pitcher. Giving his boots a final polish with the damp towel, he crossed to the small fireplace and drew aside the fender. He reached in under the fire grate and pulled out the small newspaper-wrapped parcel. Inside was the .38 Smith & Wesson automatic pistol he had been given in preparation for today's shooting. Putting on his overcoat, he shoved the weapon into the righthand pocket and put on his hat. With a final quick glance around the room he left, closing the door as silently as possible. Tip-toeing down the stairs, he continued to the front door of the hotel. There was no sign of the night porter. It was now a little before 8.00 a.m. and he had plenty of time to walk to Ely Place where he would meet the rest of the Squad.

On the way, he went over in his mind the instructions he had been given. On no account were any Volunteers to be seen near Ely Place before 8.55 a.m. There was to be no loitering to kill time on the way. They should walk around or cycle in circles if necessary. Jack decided to cross the Liffey at O'Connell Bridge and walk down the North Wall Quay. The ferryman at Spencer Dock would row him across the Liffey to Sir John Rogerson's Quay opposite. Then he recalled that the steps at the ferry were a stone's throw from a nest of Black and Tans stationed in a nearby red brick building – once a shipping company hotel. Although he had been stopped and searched now and again on passing by there, he had never had any trouble. Chatting to them as a sympathetic ex-serviceman and explaining his job as a bookie's runner always worked. But if they caught him now with a gun in his pocket he knew that, instead of crossing the Liffey he'd end up in it, floating out on the tide. Jack turned to cross the river by the swivel bridge next to the Customs House.

All in all, he didn't expect any other problems. The Auxiliary night patrols ended with the curfew at dawn, when they would be replaced by the day patrols. On a Sunday, they tended to come on the streets somewhat later. The Black and Tans would be the real threat when all the ' jobs' were done.

ooooo0000oooooo

The noise of someone outside in the corridor roused Waite from sleep. Chinks of early dawn light showed around the edges of the heavy curtains and partially dispelled the bedroom's gloom. Sitting up, he gave an involuntary groan as his muscles protested. He realised that he had slept all night in

198

the armchair. His watch indicated that it was a few minutes past seven o'clock. Rising, he stretched tentatively and then drew back the heavy curtains. Dressed and shaved, he left for the dining room and ate hungrily. When he had checked out at reception, he looked at his watch – 8.50 a.m. The curfew was well over by now so it would be safe to leave the hotel.

Outside, there were far more people about than he had expected at this time on a Sunday morning. Everything looked perfectly normal – or 'grand' as the Irish would say. A British officer came into view approaching the hotel. He seemed quite composed and indifferent to his surroundings. As passers-by headed for the nearby church, Waite found it difficult to believe that yesterday's drama had actually happened. Had he simply misunderstood Jack? But the fact remained that Jack had uttered his, Waite's, name. But, Waite decided with some relief, he had probably remembered his name having originally heard it in that Court Martial in France. Momentarily, his spirits lifted, then fell again as he recalled Jack's words. Undecided, Waite lingered on the steps of the hotel. Jack had said that he shouldn't stay in his lodgings last night. Had the danger passed? Was it now safe? Waite decided to walk over to Ely Place, not with the intention to enter his lodgings, but simply to look around the area to see if there was anything to worry about.

ooooo0000oooooo

Kate awoke cold and uncomfortable in almost pitch black darkness. She stretched out her hand. As her fingers touched cold stone, the reality of her imprisonment struck. It must have been close to three o'clock in the morning when they had finally arrived at the Castle. She concluded that she might have slept for perhaps three or four hours. It was too dark for her to see her watch. The sleep, such as it was, had helped. Yawning, she recalled being lifted on to the lorry outside her great-aunt's house by two Black and Tans and ordered to sit on the bench seat close to the driver's cab. The penetrating chill of a cold November night was numbing. The lorry's canvas covering provided little protection from the constant draughts that changed direction as it drove around the sleeping streets. As it gradually filled with arrested men, their bulk acted as a windbreak. It took hours before all the prisoners on this run were seized. And of course, being a Saturday night – or Sunday morning by then – quite a few of those detained were intoxicated.

As the prisoners, including Kate, dismounted, she recognised that they were outside Ship Street barracks on the west perimeter of Dublin Castle. One of the Auxiliary officers called out six names from a notebook he was holding – hers among them – and instructed them to stand together in a separate group. As most of the remainder of those arrested were in various stages of inebriation, she concluded that most if not all in her group were Republicans. Then, escorted by four armed soldiers with fixed bayonets, they were marched through the barracks and out its rear entrance into the Castle grounds. They crossed the inner carriageway flanking the south aspect of the Castle buildings. In the dim light of the small gaslights on its walls, she caught glimpses of armed soldiers in the shadows all the way along to the Lower Castle yard. Stopping at a solid wooden door between the Bermingham Tower and the West Gate, one of their escort tapped its small knocker. Inside, soldiers took charge of the prisoners and escorted them along a short narrow passageway lit by a bare electric bulb. Stopping at another door, one of the guards opened it with a key, and the prisoners filed in to a passageway of roughly cut stone walls with recessed doors on the left. At the first open doorway, her escort spoke. 'In you go, Miss. That's where you'll be spending what's left of the night.'

Kate had scarcely glanced about when the door slammed shut and the dim bulb above was extinguished. She had had just enough time to see what appeared to be a long timber bed held to the stone walls by support chains at each end. Crouching downwards, her hands outstretched, she moved slowly in its direction. She felt what she guessed were a couple of blankets lying on what seemed to be a thin palliasse serving as a mattress. A malodorous pillow was flat and thin with wear. Lifting the end of the mattress, she placed the pillow underneath. She could not bear to lay her head on it. With her coat buttoned and its collar turned up, she lay down and drew the blankets over herself. Her thoughts wheeled between concern for her aunt and trepidation for herself. Eventually, her breathing slowed and she fell into a fitful sleep.

Sitting up in the gloom, she swung her legs over the side of the bunk. She took off her coat and shook it in an effort to get rid of the worst of the creases, then put it on again. Clad in rumpled clothes, she felt uncomfortable and, somehow, embarrassed. The cell bulb came on. Shading her eyes in the sudden brightness, she glanced at her wrist watch. It was 8.10 a.m. Looking around, her heart sank. It was a truly dreadful place. There was no window, not even a slit aperture. Apart from her bench bed and a bucket in the corner, it was empty. Were the cells in Kilmainham and Mountjoy gaols as primitive as this? Kate tried to work out exactly where she was being held. These arched cells were certainly in the bowels of the old Castle. Were they for special prisoners? Were the underground cells in the Tower of London like this?

It struck her as odd that no one had questioned her so far. Yet interrogation was inevitable. But by whom? An Auxiliary officer? An Army officer? A detective? Whoever it might be, she was prepared. The instructions routinely given to all Sinn Féin operatives were clear: in any interrogation she was to remain mute. She was to concentrate on memorising the significant questions put to her as best she could pertaining to Dáil Éireann monies and ... a key was turning in the cell door! As it opened, a cockney voice shouted as a tin plate clanged against the outer stonework. 'Wakey, wakey! Breakfast time!'

ooooo0000ooooo

By 8.45 a.m., Jack had circled Merrion Square twice to fill in the time. Walking up Fitzwilliam Street, he turned right into Baggot Street and continued on towards the corner of Merrion Row and Ely Place. It took longer than he expected. He quickened his pace. He spotted another one of his Squad coming from the direction of the Shelbourne Hotel. They ignored one another. They had been warned that another 'job' would be taking place in the hotel and to steer clear. Turning into Ely Place, Jack paused for a moment. Members of the Squad were in place at the far end of the cul-de-sac. They seemed to be chatting among themselves, but as he drew closer he couldn't hear a sound. They looked like a group of young fellas waiting to go somewhere. But he knew they would be all wound up inside preparing themselves for the attack. Well, their man wasn't going to be there. Not unless he was a complete fool.

As Jack joined the group their unit O.C. strode up to them, hissed for attention and then spoke quietly.

'In two minutes, Joe will knock at the door. You know what you have to do?'

Jack noted that the O.C. was now looking directly at him. He nodded. He would have liked to know who wanted Lexington shot? And, more interesting, who didn't? Jack knew he'd never find out. But the one good thing about all this hugger-mugger was that Mr. Staunton and his bosses clearly trusted him. If they didn't, he reckoned he too would have been plugged by now.

The O.C. was looking at his watch. 'Fifteen seconds, men,' he murmured.

They waited, tense.

'Now!'

The first of the Squad to reach the door pulled the bell knob. A little later the door opened. A maid stood surprised and confused on being confronted by so many men. Before she got her wits together, the Squad had pushed her aside as they swept into the hallway. One of the Volunteers pushed the quaking girl ahead of him down the backstairs to the basement and into the kitchen area where the rest of the servants were clearing up after breakfast. Warning them to remain where they were, he shut the door and waited outside on guard.

Jack had been assigned to the shooting group and was first up the stairs. Other Volunteers spread out around the house to post lookouts with one guarding the back garden gate. Another remained on the front doorstep watching out for an Auxiliary patrol. Should one come into view he would go into the hall and fire a warning shot.

By now Jack's group were on the top floor landing. One of them turned the brass doorknob. Finding it locked, he fired a shot downward at the lock. The door shuddered as wood splintered. A second bullet finished the lock. The O.C. kicked the door open, motioning Jack ahead into the large bedroom-cum-sitting room. His gun cocked, Jack stopped. The bed hadn't been slept in. Mr. Lexington hadn't been stupid.

'Empty, Sir.'

'O.K, Jack, open the window and listen there.'

Following Jack inside, the O.C. groaned in frustration.

'In with you, lads. You know what to do.'

The group split up, each going about his assigned task. Jack watched as Waite's wardrobe and chest of drawers were searched and emptied on to the carpeted floor. The O.C. gave the empty waste paper basket a cursory glance before beginning his search of the writing desk. The Volunteer who had searched under the bed was now standing with a chamber pot in his hand.

'Clean as a whistle!'

'This fella is really holding out!' another Volunteer quipped.

A general titter broke the tension.

'Quiet!'

The O.C. renewed his rapid scrutiny of every sheet of paper in Waite's writing desk before throwing them on the floor. Absolutely nothing so far. This Lexington fellow was either very clever or the wrong man. He picked up the framed photograph on the chest of drawers. It showed a smiling young man flanked by an older couple, clearly his parents. The O.C. tossed it aside. Flicking through the last few pages of insurance documents, a whistle from the stairwell signalled danger. Time to go.

ooooo0OOO0ooooo

As he passed by the railings of Stephen's Green, Waite glanced across to the Shelbourne Hotel. A jarvey led his horse cab away from the kerb, revealing a group of young men who were chatting and laughing on the pavement. As though at a signal, the smokers in the group discarded their half smoked cigarettes and entered the hotel. Probably young fellows up from the country for that Irish football match in Croke Park, Waite guessed.

At the entrance to the Green, he looked inside. All that was to be seen was an elderly man with his dog on a lead. Turning, he walked across the broad pavement to the kerb. In less than a minute he was close to the corner of Ely Place.

ooooo00000ooooo

Two soldiers stood at the cell door, one with a large satchel on his left shoulder and a Webley in his right hand. The other carried a cylindrical tea urn and a tin mug. Filling the mug with what looked and smelled like tea already milked he thrust it forward.'

'Where's your mug, Miss?' he demanded.

'I don't have one.' Kate replied.

'Too bad.' Emptying the mug onto the cell floor he turned to his companion.

'Gimme a sandwich, Bob.' He offered it to Kate.

'No, thank you. I am not hungry.'

'Suit yourself, Miss, but it's all the food you'll be getting today.'

Practicality won out over squeamishness and she took it. As the cell door shut and the key rattled in the lock, she sat on the edge of the bunk with her 'breakfast.' Taking a bite, she found it almost tasteless. She prised the thick slices apart. It was just plain bread and butter. Taking another bite she changed her mind – it was margarine, not butter. As she ate, she mulled over how she might explain her present position to Stephen. She had never considered the possibility of her arrest. She belonged to a class to which arrest was unthinkable. But it had happened. Escape was clearly out of the question. When would she see Stephen again? Would he even want to see her again when he learned of her arrest and her involvement in Dáil Éireann work? He might well be so shocked as to have no further interest in her.

The fact remained she was under arrest. Worse, the authorities knew not only her name but also that she was staying with her aunt. Had she been over-confident? Or worse, had she been careless? With a sinking feeling, Kate knew that she faced the reality of, at best, a two-year sentence, more than likely in the notorious Holloway Prison for women in London. Her colleague, Miss Magrane, was being held there. She too had been arrested in a surprise raid on her Dawson Street flat where the Auxiliaries had seized incriminating documents – Dáil Éireann papers. Kate was under no illusion that the fact that nothing had been found in her Aunt's house would attest to her innocence. Last night, that officer had said that Mr O'Brien was also under arrest. She wondered how that frail old man would cope with rough questioning. But above all, she was most concerned for Mama and Father and their shock and embarrassment on learning of her arrest.

ooooo00000ooooo

'Time up! Out now, lads. Disperse as instructed.'

The stair carpet muffled the sound of their boots. As the Volunteers passed the lookout on the doorsteps and ran down Ely Place, they scattered, some running across to St. Stephen's Green, others towards Merrion Street. The O.C. stopped. 'Thanks for the warning, Brendan. What was it?'

'I thought I heard gunshots.'

'You probably did.' The O.C. grinned. 'There's another job on Upper Pembroke Street. Eleven Volunteers out?'

'Yes, Sir, I counted them. You're the last.'

ooooo0000oooooo

Waite had barely turned into Ely Place when a group of men raced past him towards Baggot Street. His eyes widened when he saw that some of them were pocketing guns. Shocked, he stopped in mid-step then instinctively continued walking. Any show of curiosity now would be madness. Eyes intent on a polished brass nameplate outside a doorway across the street, he strode toward it, ignoring the last of the young men jogging passed him.

Jack, running with the group making for Baggot Street, couldn't believe it was Lexington ahead. What a gom! After all the trouble he took to warn him. Well, Sir, you're on your own now, he thought. Slowing, he watched the fool walking to the opposite pavement where he was confronted by the O.C.

'Stop or I'll shoot!'

The gun barrel inches from his head, Waite froze. 'I beg your pardon?'

The gunman peered at him then grinned triumphantly. 'You're the lad in the photograph! You're Lexington!'

'Yes ... No, NO! Waite's the na ... '

Waite was dead before the noise of the Webley's shot reached his eardrums. His body slumping backwards onto the roadway, his hat still in place, he lay prone on the cobbles.

'Bloody fool!' Jack shook his head as he ran on.

ooooo0000Oooooo

The noise of the cell door being unlocked startled Kate. She jumped to her feet. Armed soldiers stood in the doorway. 'You're to come with us, Miss,' one of them said.

'Where are you taking me?' Kate asked.

'You'll see soon enough.'

They climbed a set of steep stone steps dimly lit by gas mantle lights and emerged into the Upper Yard at, as she had guessed, the south west corner. The surrounding two-storey brick buildings housed the centre of British administrative power in Ireland. The Throne Room, St. Patrick's Hall and other chambers for state events were behind the modest pillared portico of the Castle's red brick south wing. Not quite opposite the portico was the arched Castle Street gate and to its left the Offices of the Garter King at Arms. All the rest of the buildings in the Upper Yard she knew housed the higher civil servants, military and police officials of the British Administration in Ireland – or as it was officially called - the 'Government of Ireland.' Walking with care across the cobbled surface between her guards, she glanced up at the statue of blind *Justitia* dominating the arch of Castle Street Gate. The constant butt of Dublin wags, it looked inwards with its back to the city's populace, unlike its sister monument gracing London's Old Bailey.

The soldiers halted at one of the doors in the office building at the other side of the gate.

'It's the second door, Len.'

'Are you sure?'

'Yes.'

Inside, a narrow hallway led to a staircase.

'I'll go up and tell him she's here.'

'O.K.'

Within minutes, Kate was sitting before a bare desk behind which a slim middle-aged man sat. He was engrossed in an open manila folder. Giving her a brief glance, he returned his attention to the file. He wore a neatly-tailored grey flannel suit with white shirt and regimental tie. His dark hair was brushed flat with a patent sheen. A thin black leather cord attached his monocle to his lapel. His face was somewhat familiar. Kate had seen him before. But where? When?

Behind his desk, a line of timber filing cabinets filled the wall from one side to the other. On her left, daylight flooded into the room from high windows. There was no other furniture. An electric light bulb with a green 'coolie hat' shade hung from the middle of the ceiling. The heat from the burning coals in the fireplace gave out a little warmth.

He closed the manila file.

'I am Colonel Winter, Chief of Police in Ireland and I report directly to General Tudor who is Special Police Adviser to the Lord Lieutenant,' he said. 'You have been detained under the provisions of the recently enacted Restoration of Order in Ireland Act. We know you have been engaged in blatant violations of the... em, the currency Acts in London on behalf of certain proclaimed organisations here in Ireland. Do you understand what I am saying, Miss Swanton?'

Kate stared at him levelly. He waited.

'So - yet another young Shinner woman mute of malice, as was the Magrane woman.' His voice was entirely without expression. 'However, we will see about that when I have a report on the search of your parent's home. This is being done even as I speak.'

Remaining impassive, Kate knew nothing incriminating would be found there. Nevertheless, such a search would profoundly shock her parents.

'My next question ...'

The telephone rang. Colonel Winter, clearly vexed, grasped the pedestal. 'I distinctly said no telephone calls for half an hour ... what? Are you certain? When? How many? Where?'

Kate saw the colour in his face drain away.

'Are you certain of that number?'

A pause.

'Then find out exactly what it is. We shall have to have an emergency meeting at twelve noon. Get in touch with Generals Tudor and Boyd, Colonel Wilson and the Divisional

Commissioner RIC, Dublin District. Oh, and yes, I suppose the R.I.C. Inspector General and the DMP Commissioner as well. And don't forget Sturgis. What! O'Connor? No point. Inform Cope. He'll be there. General Macready is in Biarritz or somewhere in southern France. Find out exactly where he is from his A.D.C. and I'll have a wire sent to him immediately. What? Yes! I'm on my way now.'

Rising, he crossed the floor. Opening the door he shouted down the stairs.

'Sergeant, take this prisoner back to her cell and put her on the list for Kilmainham Prison.'

Returning, he stood beside her. 'Miss Swanton, you will not be seeing me again. In the next few days you will be escorted to Holloway Prison in London. There you will join the Magrane woman – another one of Mr. Collins's coven – for the foreseeable future. Good day to you!'

Seated again on the plank bed in her cell, Kate stared unseeing at the wall. Her thoughts were in turmoil. Concern for her aunt and for her parents jostled with dread at the thought of how Stephen would react when he learned of her duplicity. Recalling the respect he had always shown towards her, the total attention he gave to her slightest utterance and, most of all, the tenderness with which he had kissed her the night before, a sob broke from her. For a few minutes, she yielded to her grief. Then she pulled herself together. Stephen was a soldier – well, he had been a soldier. He would understand that it was necessary to carry out one's duty and that she herself was as duty-bound as any soldier. She brightened. And now that everything was in the open and there were no more secrets, they would be free to love each other without reservation. She was sure of it.

The key rattled in the door. Kate stood.